STAR WARS FORCES OF DESTINY™

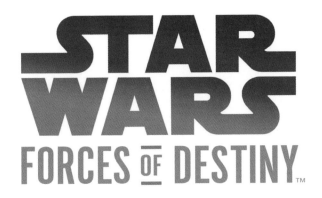

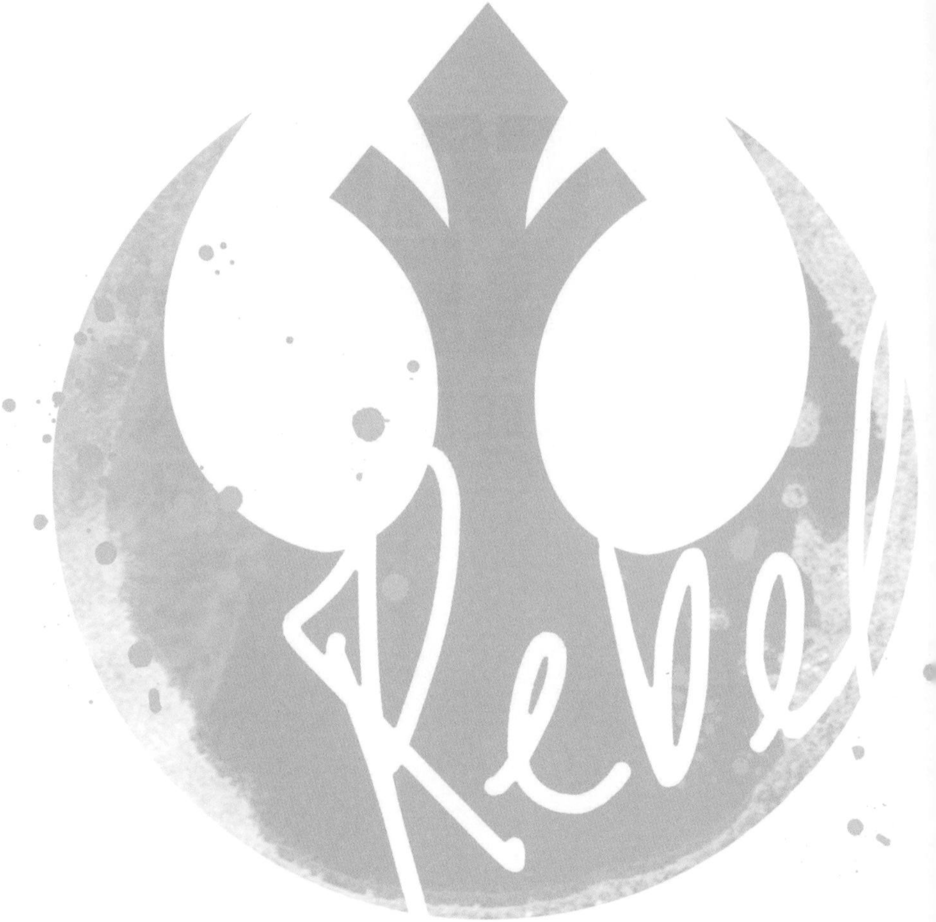
Rebel

STAR WARS
FORCES OF DESTINY™

The Leia Chronicles

Written by
Emma Carlson Berne

Disney
LUCASFILM
PRESS
Los Angeles • New York

ABDO
Spotlight

ABDOBOOKS.COM

Reinforced library bound edition published in 2020 by Spotlight, a division of ABDO
PO Box 398166, Minneapolis, Minnesota 55439. Spotlight produces high-quality
reinforced library bound editions for schools and libraries.
Published by agreement with Disney • Lucasfilm Press.

Printed in the United States of America, North Mankato, Minnesota.
042019
092019

THIS BOOK CONTAINS
RECYCLED MATERIALS

PRESS

Library of Congress Control Number: 2018966041

Publisher's Cataloging-in-Publication Data

Names: Carlson Berne, Emma, author. | Disney–Lucasfilm Press, illustrator.
Title: The Leia chronicles / by Emma Carlson Berne; illustrated by Disney–Lucasfilm
    Press.
Description: Minneapolis, Minnesota : Spotlight, 2020. | Series: Star Wars: forces of
    destiny chapter books
Summary: Follow Leia as she undertakes a dangerous mission, makes some cuddly
    new friends, and protects an unlikely group of prisoners.
Identifiers: ISBN 9781532143274 (lib. bdg.)
Subjects: LCSH: Star wars, forces of destiny (Television program)--Juvenile fiction. |
    Organa, Leia (Fictitious character)--Juvenile fiction. | Rescue work--Juvenile
    fiction. | Adventure stories--Juvenile fiction. | Space--Juvenile fiction. | Comic
    books, strips, etc--Juvenile fiction.
Classification: DDC [FIC]--dc23

Spotlight
A Division of ABDO
abdobooks.com

CONTENTS

A MESSAGE FROM MAZ

Come here, friend. I'll show you how the water rushes through the dark banks of the river. You can hear the roaring if you listen. But be careful! Light your way with this torch. What? Why do you stand there? I see you hear my words, yet you do not move? Do you trust me? Ah. I see now. Trust is hard to gain, easy to lose. Trusting creatures you have just met. Trusting that you can make a bad situation better—if only you stand your ground. Trusting

that someone else will work just as hard for
a cause as you will. Trusting a new friend
that she won't let you slip into the river. Once
you do trust, though, well then—you might be
surprised at how brave you can be. Here—take
my hand. I'll hold the torch high. Step closer.

Trust me. And remember, the choices we
make, the actions we take, the moments—both
big and small—shape us into forces of destiny.

EWOK ESCAPE

Leia clambered over another massive fallen
tree, her muscles still twinging from the
fight with the stormtrooper. The furry, fierce
little creature who'd helped her toddled
determinedly ahead. He appeared to be on the
verge of toppling over with every step, but his
round little body was surprisingly effective at
navigating the massive trees, tangled vines,

and moss-covered boulders that littered the forest moon of Endor.

"Hey!" She wove her way between two huge boulders rearing up from the soil and caught up with the Ewok. "Thanks for helping me out back there." The furry animal turned around. His face was appealingly smushed, with a stubby black nose. He was completely covered in fur, but he wore a roughly cut hood over his head and shoulders, and carried a wooden staff topped with a stone spearhead. Leia had already seen how sharp the spear was, when he'd jabbed the stormtrooper trying to capture her just a few minutes before. Now there she was—speeder bike wrecked, her friends Luke, Han, and Chewbacca probably looking for her, stormtroopers everywhere—being led along by something that looked like a stuffed toy holding a spear.

The mission had begun when the Rebel Alliance discovered that the Empire was constructing another Death Star, orbiting the forest moon of Endor. The second Death Star wasn't complete, but it was protected by a powerful shield. To destroy the Death Star, an advance team needed to land on the forest moon and disable the generator that was powering the shield.

That was where Leia and the others had come in.

She, Han, Luke, and Chewie, along with the droids C-3PO and R2-D2 and some rebel soldiers, had boarded a stolen Imperial shuttle and taken it to Endor, slipping past Imperial guards on the moon. That was all very well and good, except the forest was crawling with stormtroopers.

Chewie and Han confronted one pair of troopers while more troopers took off on their speeder bikes. Leia and Luke jumped on another bike, leaving Han and Chewie behind, and zoomed through the forest, chasing after the troopers. Leia steered their speeder up next to a trooper's and Luke jumped onto it, throwing the trooper off.

Using his lightsaber to

deflect blaster fire, Luke took out at least one more trooper before Leia lost sight of him. She and another trooper exchanged fire before he clipped the tail of her speeder, sending her flying headfirst toward the ground. Luckily, she shook off the impact in time to see the trooper drive his speeder directly into a giant fallen tree, where it burst into flames.

Bruised and aching, with her head ringing from the crash, she let herself relax on a bed of springy moss, and with her cheek pressed against the damp ground, she fell unconscious.

The next thing she knew, she was being poked in the side by something sharp. She jolted awake to see the little furry creature, spear at the ready. He danced around, threatening her, clearly suspicious. It was hard not to laugh at him; he was so little, yet clearly so tough. She sat on a log, resting, and took off her helmet. He chattered at her in alarm. "You're a jittery little thing," she told him, and showed him that the helmet was just a hat. Food was always good to build trust, she'd found, so she offered him some of her rations to eat. That seemed to win him over, and it was a good thing, too, because the Ewok was smarter than he looked.

Together, they had fought off two stormtroopers who'd found them soon after. The creature bashed one in the knee so Leia could finish him off, then she blasted the second one as the trooper tried to escape on his speeder.

At least she could breathe for a second now

that it was all over. Leia craned her neck to admire the massive trees towering into the filtered sunlight. She hadn't been able to fully appreciate the splendor while she was being shot at by stormtroopers and riding a speeder.

Then Leia bent down to the Ewok. "Look, I appreciate all your help, but I need to find my friends."

His black eyes glittered. He jerked his spear forward and gestured insistently.

Suddenly, voices came from up ahead— high and squeaky, then loud. The Ewok halted, throwing his stubby arm across Leia's legs. He pointed toward the sound, then took off running through the forest. He chattered at her over his shoulder.

"Wait!" Leia ran after him. "Come back

here!" She wove among the massive tree trunks, vines reaching down to brush her shoulders as hanging branches almost hit her in the face. Suddenly, the Ewok skidded to a halt and she nearly trampled him. He gestured and she saw the gleam of shiny white through the green-and-brown gloom.

"Stormtroopers," she whispered to him, and he nodded, holding his spear at the ready.

Cautiously, they crept forward. The Ewok motioned Leia down behind a boulder. She dropped to the spongy damp ground and peered cautiously around the rock.

Two stormtroopers loomed over two Ewoks. The little creatures wore the same rough hoods as her new Ewok friend and had finely woven baskets over their arms,

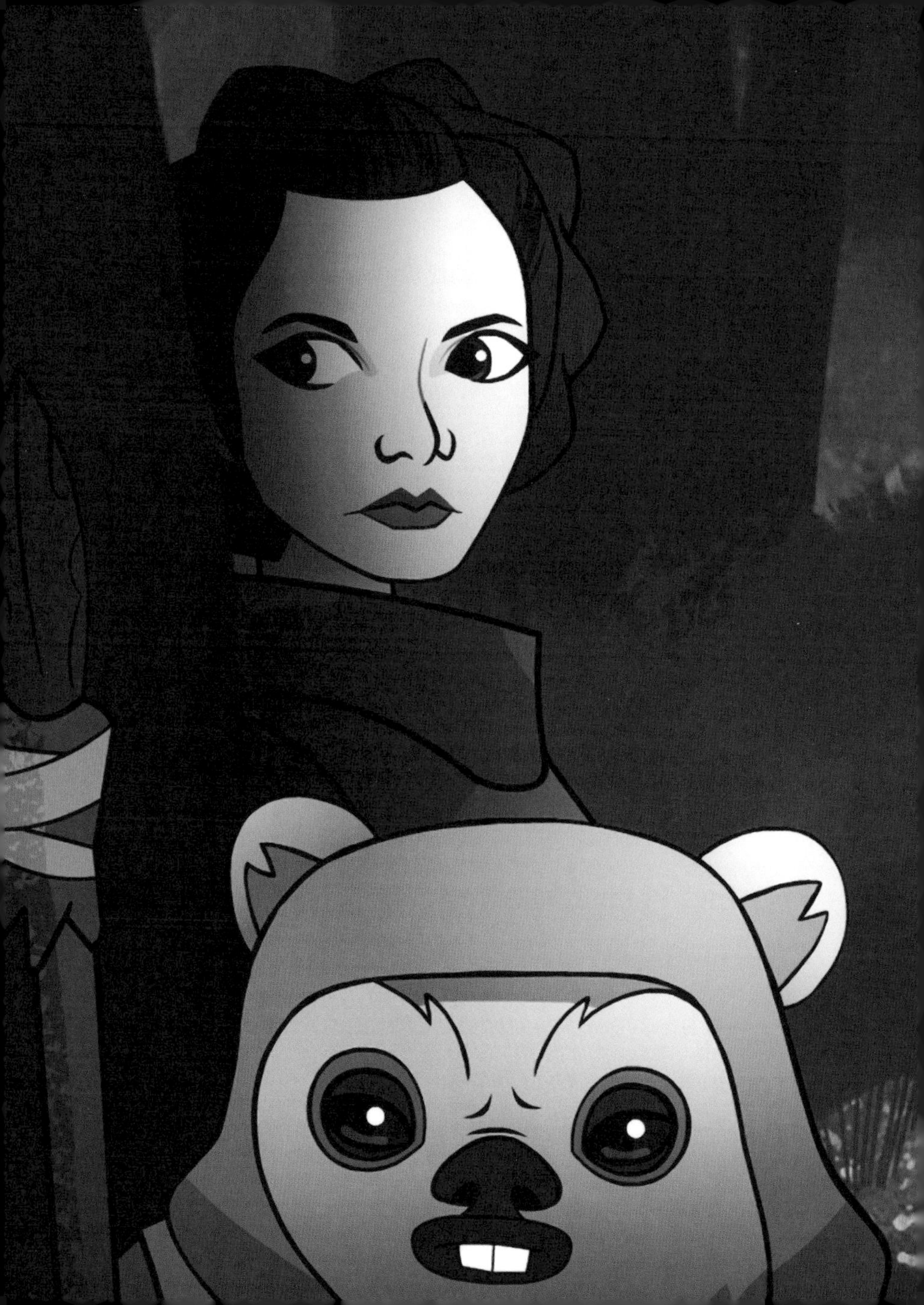

filled with some kind of round purple fruit. The Ewoks chattered, gesturing wildly. They backed away from the troopers, clearly hoping to escape. Then the troopers grasped the creatures by the necks and pushed them roughly to the ground.

"We have to help your friends," Leia whispered to the Ewok.

But the space beside her was empty.

"Huh?" Leia sat up, looking around. Then she spotted a furry form moving up one of the trees as nimbly as a tooka cat. "What are you doing?" Leia hissed, crawling over to the Ewok on her forearms.

The creature didn't answer. Leia held her breath as the Ewok reached an upper branch and began carefully making his way across. The thin branch was shiny and slick with rain and moss. The creature stepped out a little farther. Then a little more. Suddenly, he slipped, wobbled, waved his arms. Leia gasped, her hand over her mouth, just as the Ewok grabbed another branch.

In the clearing, the troopers were standing over their prizes, with the little creatures cowering at their feet. "Can you believe it?" one said. "These things are everywhere. Primitives. I'm surprised the Empire didn't deal with them when we arrived."

Suddenly, one of the Ewoks on the ground, a mottled gray one, looked up and stiffened. Leia winced. The Ewok had caught sight of Leia's

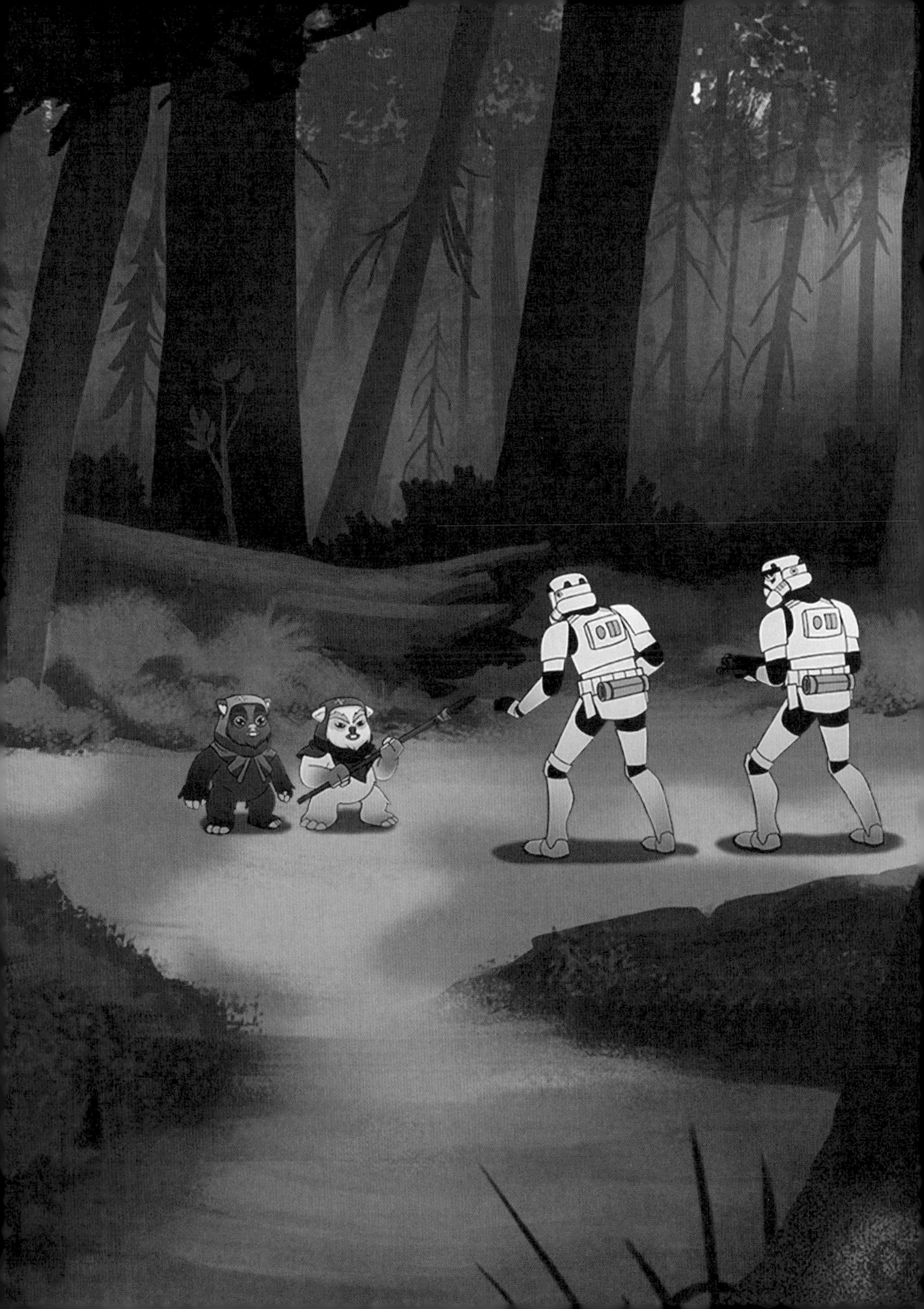

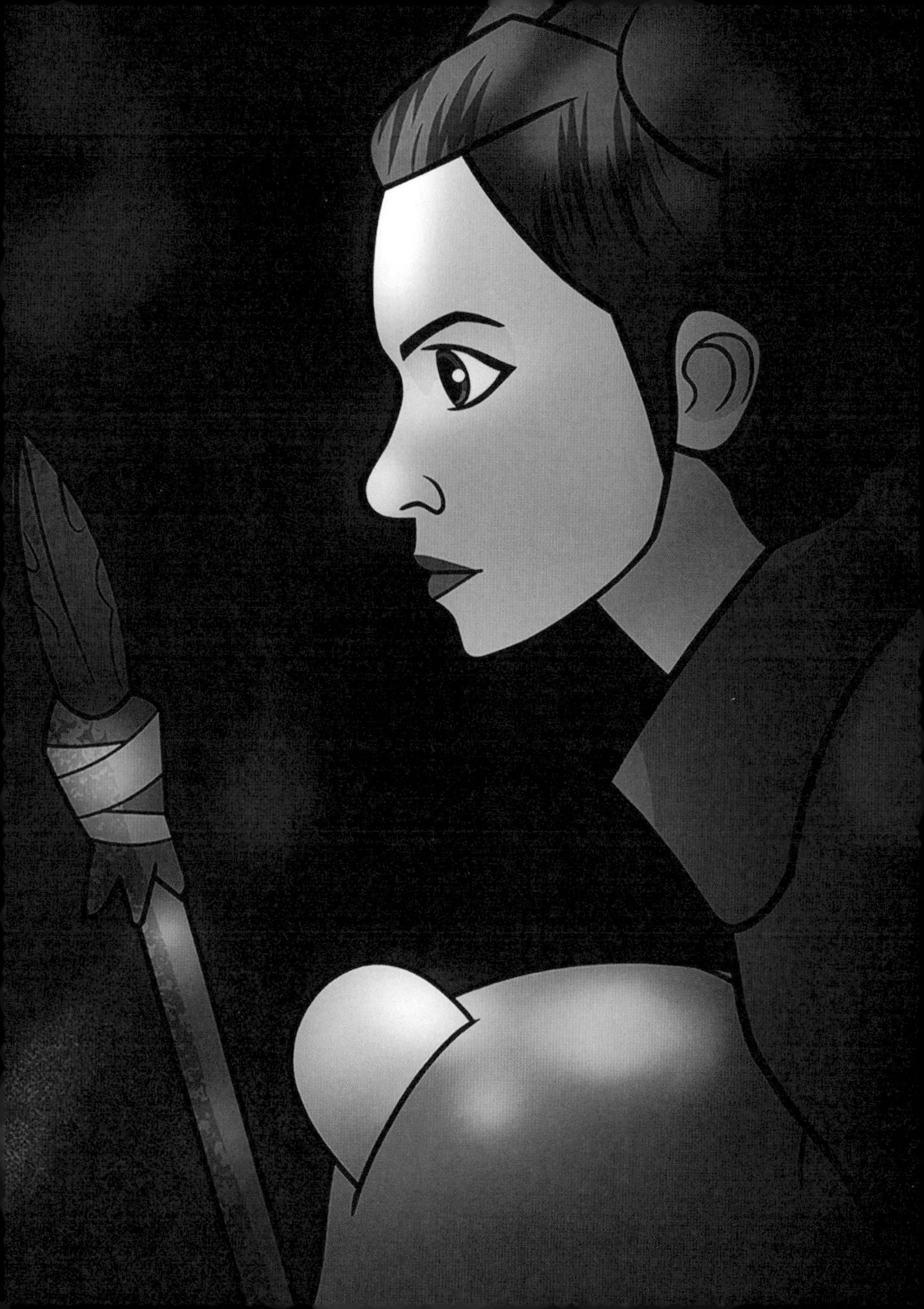

new friend on the branch. *Don't give him away, don't give him away. . . .* As she watched, the small brown Ewok jumped from one branch to another.

The trooper saw that one of the Ewoks was carrying a small spear and grabbed it from the creature. "Is this a weapon?" He shoved the gray Ewok back to the ground. The Ewok grunted with the impact of the shove and the other Ewok moved to help.

Leia watched, riveted, as her buddy drew a rough stone knife from a pouch at his waist and slashed two thick hanging vines with expert ease. "Ah! Smart little guy." Leia smiled to herself. He was going to lay a trap.

The creature deftly tied the vines into a lasso. He released the loop, which snaked fast toward the ground, dropping neatly over the troopers and encircling their bodies.

"Hey!" one of them yelled. "What? Whoa!" He pinwheeled his arms to keep his balance.

The Ewok jumped onto the dangling end of the vines, clinging to it with his nimble strong hands, and slid to the ground, yanking the stormtroopers on the other end up into the air. The captured Ewoks applauded approvingly.

But something was going wrong. Leia saw that the Ewok wasn't heavy enough to keep the stormtroopers high above the ground. The burly troopers squirmed and kicked. Leia grimaced as the Ewok slowly rose into the air on his end of the vine until he was face-to-face with the troopers.

For an instant, the troopers stared at the

Ewok in disbelief as he dangled from the vine not two meters from their faces.

"Hey!" one of the troopers shouted. "Blast him!"

The other trooper managed to pull his blaster and fire off a shot. The Ewok did the splits, narrowly avoiding it. The Ewoks on the ground sent up a storm of furious chattering.

He needs my help, Leia realized. The Ewok had done pretty well against two troopers three times his size, armed with blasters, but he might need a bit of assistance.

Leia leapt out from behind the boulder, and quickly, before the trapped troopers could realize what was happening, she made a running jump and grabbed the vine from which the Ewok was hanging.

With a hissing, sliding sound, the troopers swooped upward, pulled by Leia's extra weight, and smacked both their helmets on the overhead branch with a *thwack*. The vine released just as quickly, and the troopers plunged back toward the ground as if involuntarily rappelling, this time landing in a messy vine-entangled heap on the forest floor.

Leia leapt down off the vine, her friend right behind her. Leia caught her breath and wiped the sweat from her forehead. Hands on her hips, she and the Ewok surveyed the stormtrooper pile in front of them.

"Nice work," Leia said.

The two captured Ewoks met Leia and her Ewok friend at the bottom of the tree. Taking care not to tread on the unconscious troopers, the three creatures led Leia through the forest, wending their way among the tree trunks, one on each side holding her hand and one leading. Leia strained her eyes through the trees, but all she saw was endless giant trunks, misty green light filtering through the branches, boulders, moss, ferns.

At last, the creatures stopped. Leia looked around. More trees. More ferns. "How far is your village from here? I appreciate your help, but I need to find my friends." Leia looked at her Ewok friend closely, hoping he understood.

But he was gesturing wildly toward the sky. Leia looked up.

There, far above her head, a beautiful village soared, with huts, bridges, fences, all perched as if by magic in the treetops. Furry creatures trotted to and fro, calling to each other, carrying piles of cloth, baskets, and bundles of sticks. As Leia watched, a group of young creatures swung across the clearing on vines, their high-pitched laughter echoing through the trees. Her friend held out his hand and gestured again. His meaning was unmistakable.

They were going up.

At the top of the tree ladder, Leia paused. She could see the village better from up there. Long rope-and-stick bridges were strung from tree to tree. Platforms around the treetops supported groups of huts. Here and there,

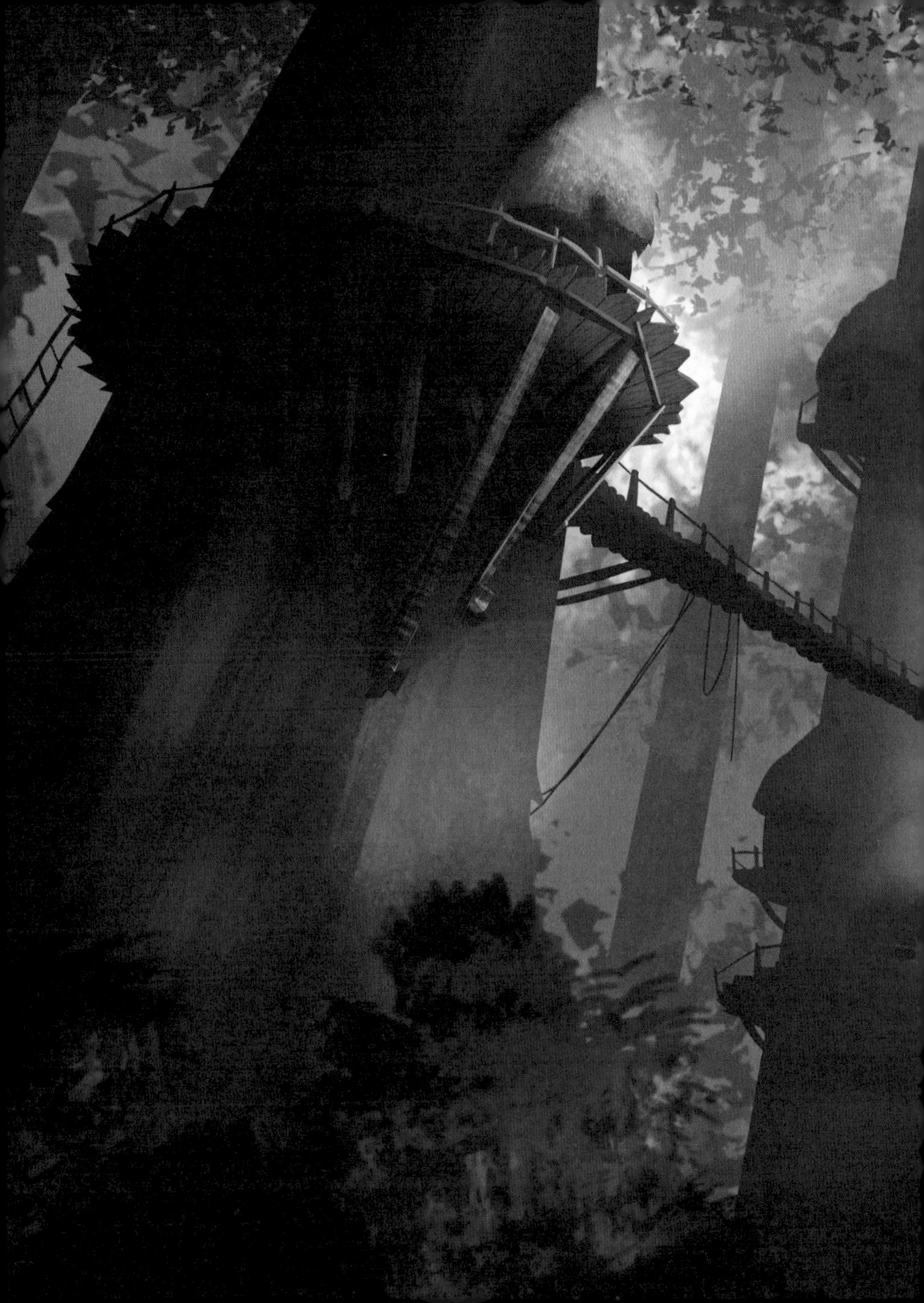

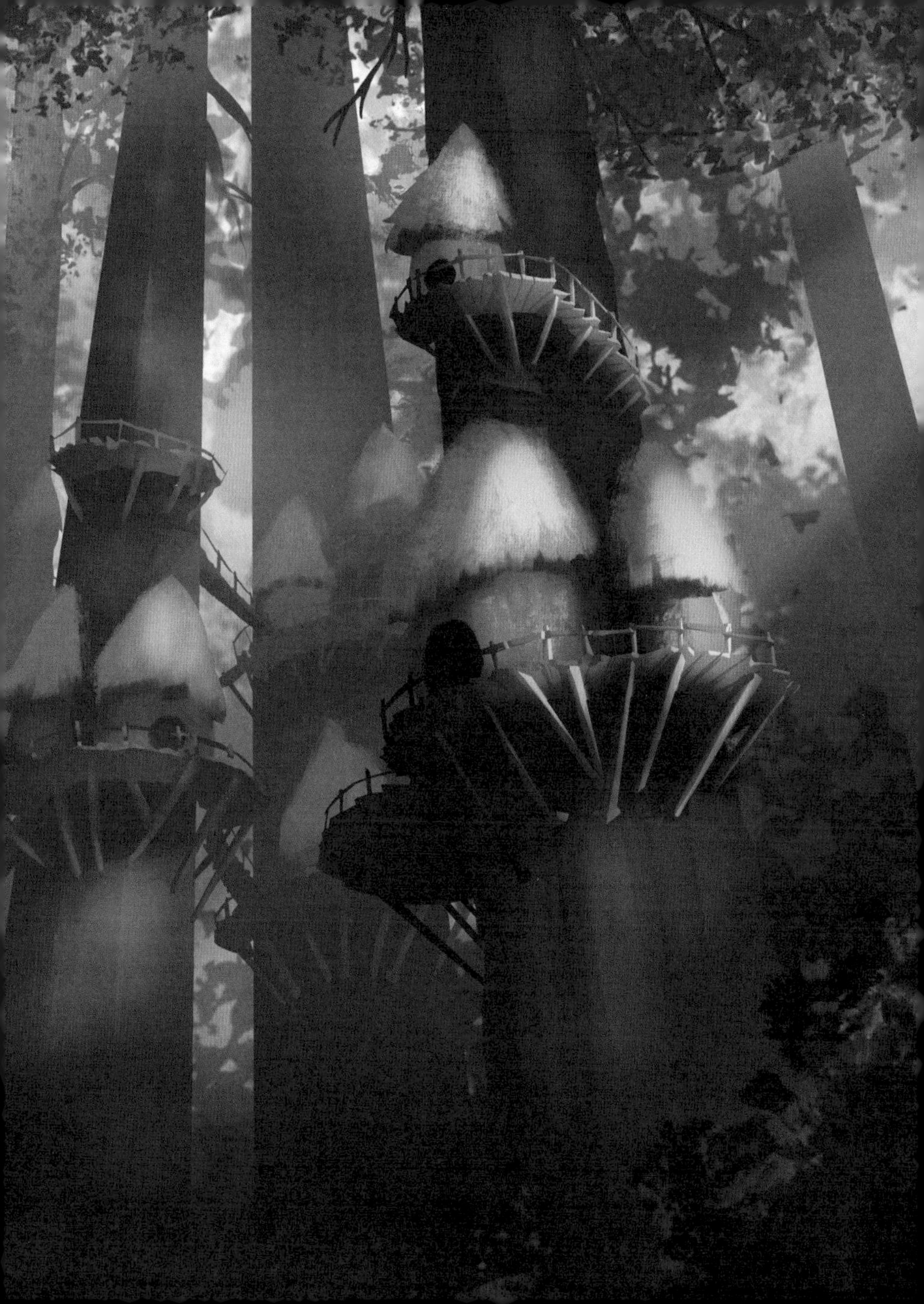

cook fires burned, with more of the creatures bent over them, stirring pots. Other groups sat in circles, weaving baskets, while outside a nearby hut, Leia could see a group of creatures skinning some sort of wild animal. Here and there, Leia glimpsed a tiny baby in a basket slung across its mother's shoulders, the little head poking out of the top, all big eyes and fuzzy fur.

A group of children ran up, surrounding them, chattering and staring with shiny black eyes. "Hey," Leia greeted them. She held out her hands. The children chattered louder, nudging each other and laughing.

Her friend said something to them sternly, then made a shooing gesture. The children scattered, shouting to each other, as slowly, ponderously, a larger Ewok approached. His fur was gray and his hood more elaborately made than her little friend's. His brows were creased, giving him a serious expression, and he held a staff made from a large bone wrapped in cloth.

As the larger Ewok approached, Leia's Ewok friend bent his head and poked her, motioning that she should do the same. Leia obeyed. Who knew what these creatures were or what they had in mind for her, but two things were for sure: one, they were excellent warriors, if her friend's skill with a spear and a snare were any indication, and two, they deserved her respect.

The larger creature—she sensed he was

the chief—chattered to her friend. The chief's meaning was clear enough: *Who is this, and why is she here?*

Her friend answered, gesturing with his spear toward the forest, then mimicking stabbing the first stormtrooper and then running, then snaring the other two. He pointed to Leia, still chattering, then took her hand and held it out to the chief.

Leia raised her head cautiously. The last thing she wanted was to somehow show disrespect to the creature. "Yes," she said. "He tells the truth. We worked together to save your people."

The chief looked her in the eye. She looked back at him. Somehow, she sensed it would be wrong if she looked away. For a long moment, he held her gaze.

Then suddenly, the chief shouted something to his village, raising his stubby arms high. He shook his staff, then gestured at Leia.

What? What was he saying? Did she do something wrong? Then her friend patted her arm reassuringly and chattered, pointing around them. Leia caught her breath. The villagers were flowing toward them, surrounding Leia, their chatter filling the air. They pressed up against her, warm and furry and solid, rubbing the fabric of her poncho, examining her fingernails, fiddling with her blaster belt.

Then one of them shouted something, and as one body, they began to move her along the rope bridge, ushering her across the rickety boards. "Okay, okay!" Leia said. "I'll stay, but only for a little while." Luke and Han and Chewie were out there—somewhere—and they might be hurt. She shoved that thought aside. Either way, she had to find them. Food, rest, and then she'd set out again. Vaguely, she wondered what else was on this moon. Furry creatures, yes, stormtroopers, yes—but what else might she find among the trees? Best to be fully rested and armed before she ventured out to find her friends.

Clinging to the ropes, trying not to slide off the slippery boards the creatures seemed to navigate so easily, she allowed herself to be nudged along until they reached what looked like a central hut on one of the platforms. It was larger than the others, and a lovely fire burned in front of it. Leia lowered herself to the ground. She arranged herself cross-legged and held her hands out to the friendly crackling flames. The forest air was damp and chilly, and the heat from the fire felt good on her face. Her Ewok buddy—apparently in some role as her host, since he had found her—settled on the ground across from her and nodded approvingly.

A rough wooden cup was pushed into her hands, and a child approached carrying a bowl heaped with purple fruits. Bowing low, with a kind of murmuring repetitive chanting, the creatures backed away, making "eat, drink" gestures.

Leia looked around at the ring of gleaming eyes and flat furry faces in the dusky twilight. She felt like she should make a speech or something; after all, it was clear she was their guest. She held the cup toward them. "Thank you." Her voice rang out over the crowd. "I am honored to be a part of your tribe." Was that right? No one seemed to take offense. Of course, they probably couldn't understand a word she was saying. Anyway, it seemed to be the right thing to say, because the chattering turned approving and numerous little hands poked out from the crowd and patted her on the back and arms.

The cup was full of a smoky-tasting brew—
probably some kind of tea—and as Leia sipped
it, she felt herself relaxing. Soon—too soon,
really—the cup was empty and a group of
creatures tugged her to her feet. They led her
to a nearby hut, pushing back the hide door and
gesturing her inside.

It was dim and warm in there. Baskets
and stone tools hung on the rough walls and
a sleeping mat lay in the corner, covered with
furs. Murmuring to each other, the Ewoks
helped Leia lie down on the mat, which
was deliciously soft. They covered her with
another fur. Oh, it was lovely. Very soft and
very nice. Much better than sleeping on piles
of leaves out in the forest. Leia felt a wave of
affection for these little creatures, whoever

they were—apparently brave, clever, and kind, which really was a winning combination.

One of them was bathing her face with something warm and damp. She smelled a sweet oil. Their murmuring was so soothing— like a lullaby. . . .

The hut was full dark when she awoke sometime later, and the creatures had gone. Leia pushed herself up, wincing at the stiffness in her muscles from the speeder crash. Leia pushed back the hide door and squeezed out.

The village was quiet, with just a few Ewoks moving around the fires, which sent plumes of fragrant smoke up through the trees. Leia sighed at the quiet peace and leaned over the railing, feeling the damp forest air on her face.

A sound made her look around. Her friend and two others were approaching. Her friend chattered, indicating something the other two were holding.

"What?" Leia asked. "Do you want to give me something?"

The Ewoks nodded, chattering, and held up what looked like a folded piece of cloth. It unfurled and Leia saw a woven dress in a soft brown material—simple but beautiful.

"Is that for me?" She smiled at them.

The Ewoks nodded and pushed the dress into her hands, shoving her back toward the hut she'd slept in.

Inside, Leia pulled the dress over her head and smoothed out the wrinkles. It fit perfectly. She heard the throbbing of drums. The glow

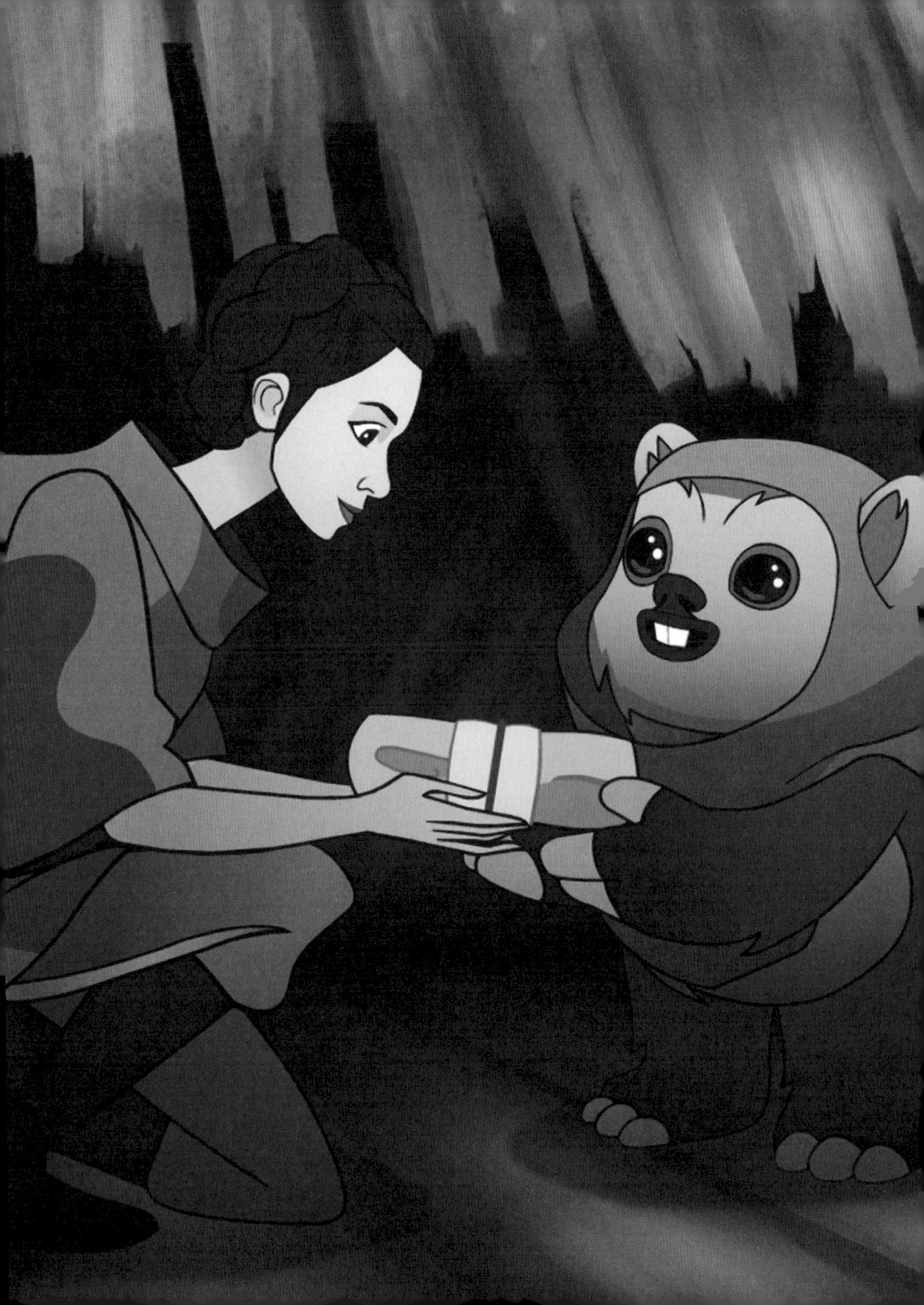

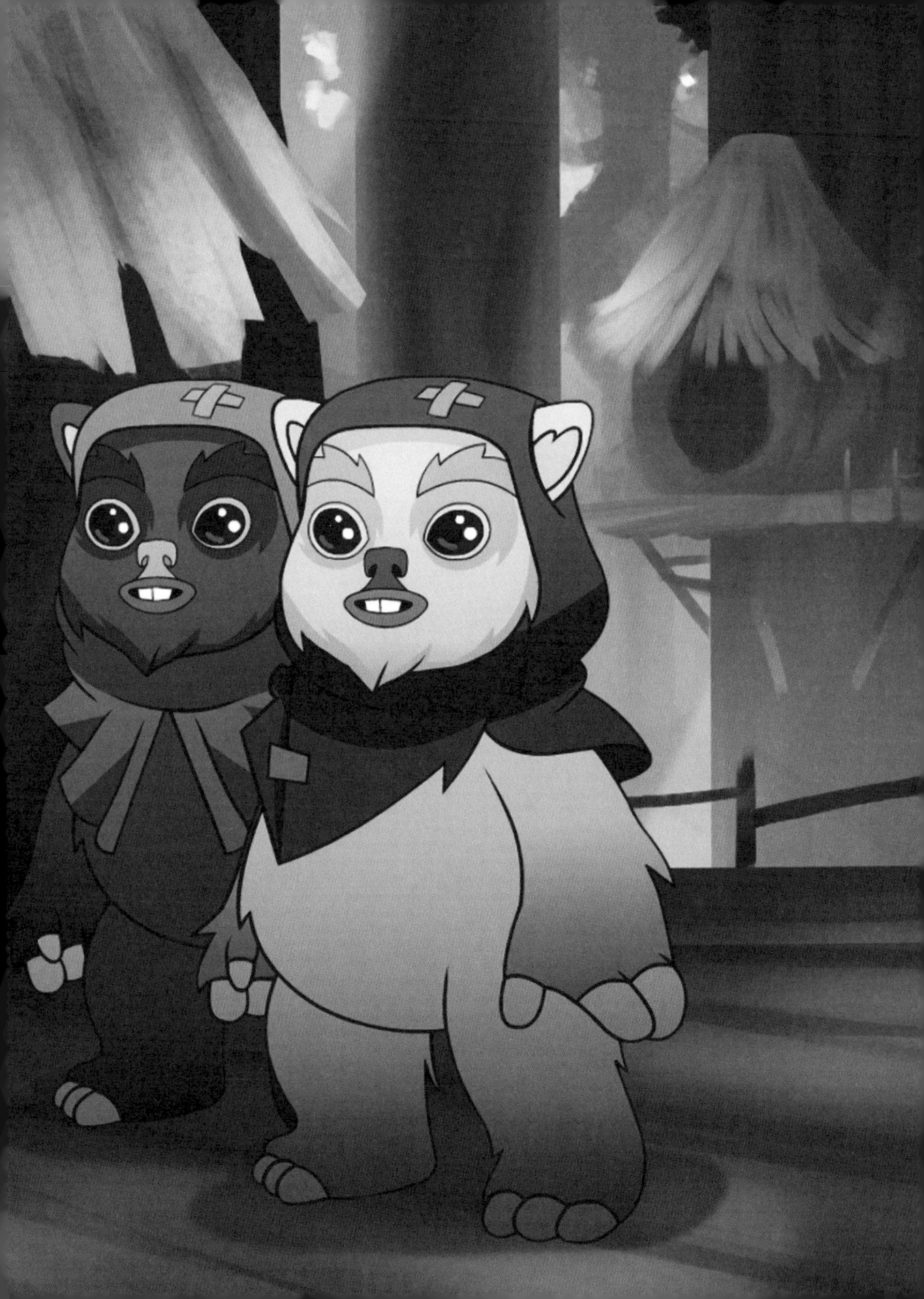

of the fire grew stronger around the edges of the hide door. Strange yips and squeals came from nearby, and above it all, she heard the high, thrilling call of a horn blowing through the treetops. The party had begun—and it was time to make her appearance.

She bent down and pushed aside the door, stepping out onto the platform. The creatures surrounded her, making little *oooh* noises, looking up at her admiringly. Leia smiled back at them all.

"Thank you for taking care of me. And thank you for this dress—I love it." They nodded, bobbing up and down, murmuring pleasantly.

She eyed her friend and the other Ewoks

nearby. They still carried their spears slung on their backs.

"But I have just one more request," she said. "Does the dress come with a spear?" She made a thrusting motion.

Her buddy chattered in response and stepped forward. He handed her his spear.

Leia held it up. "I think it's perfect!"

The Ewoks broke into giggles as Leia smiled.

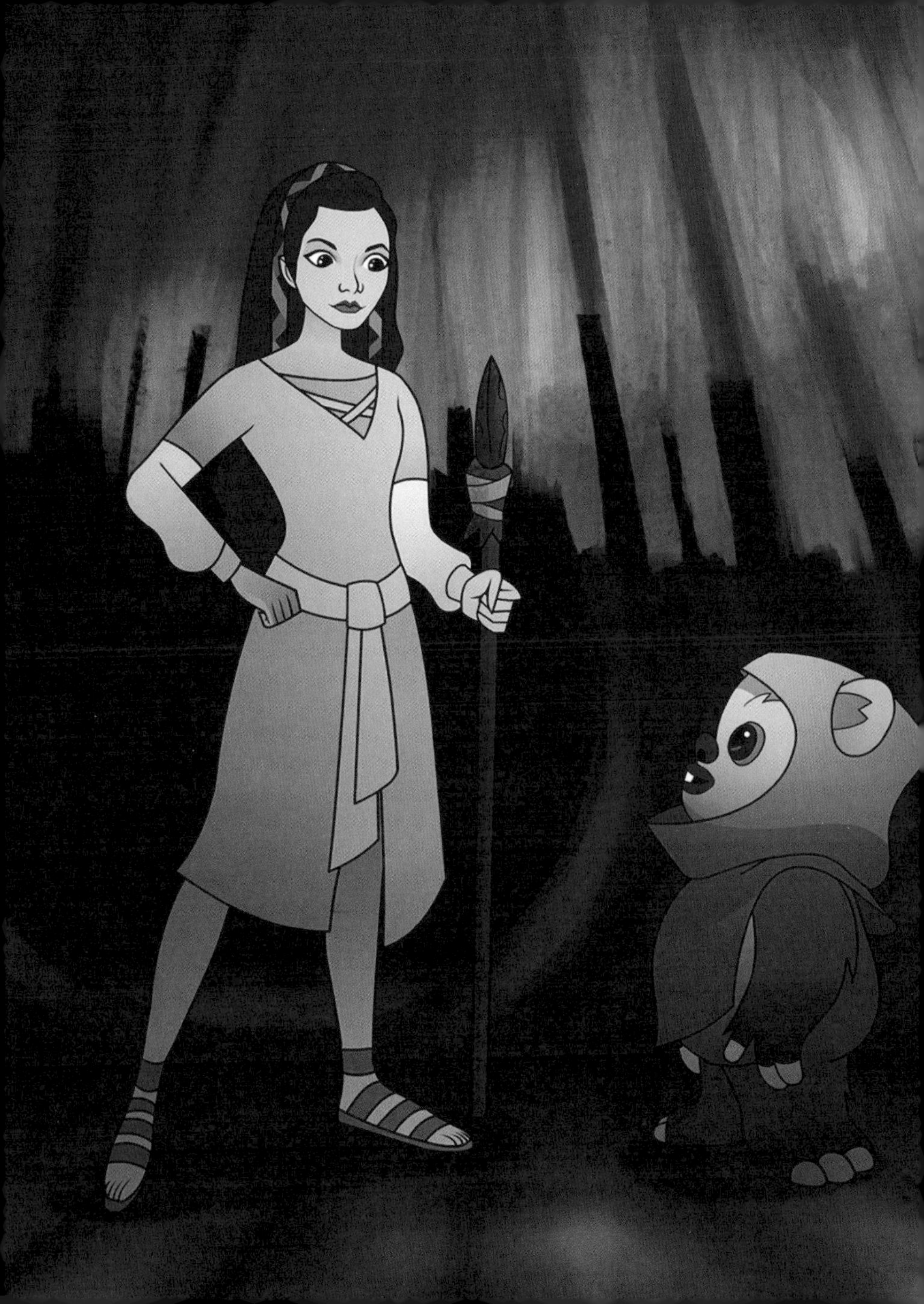

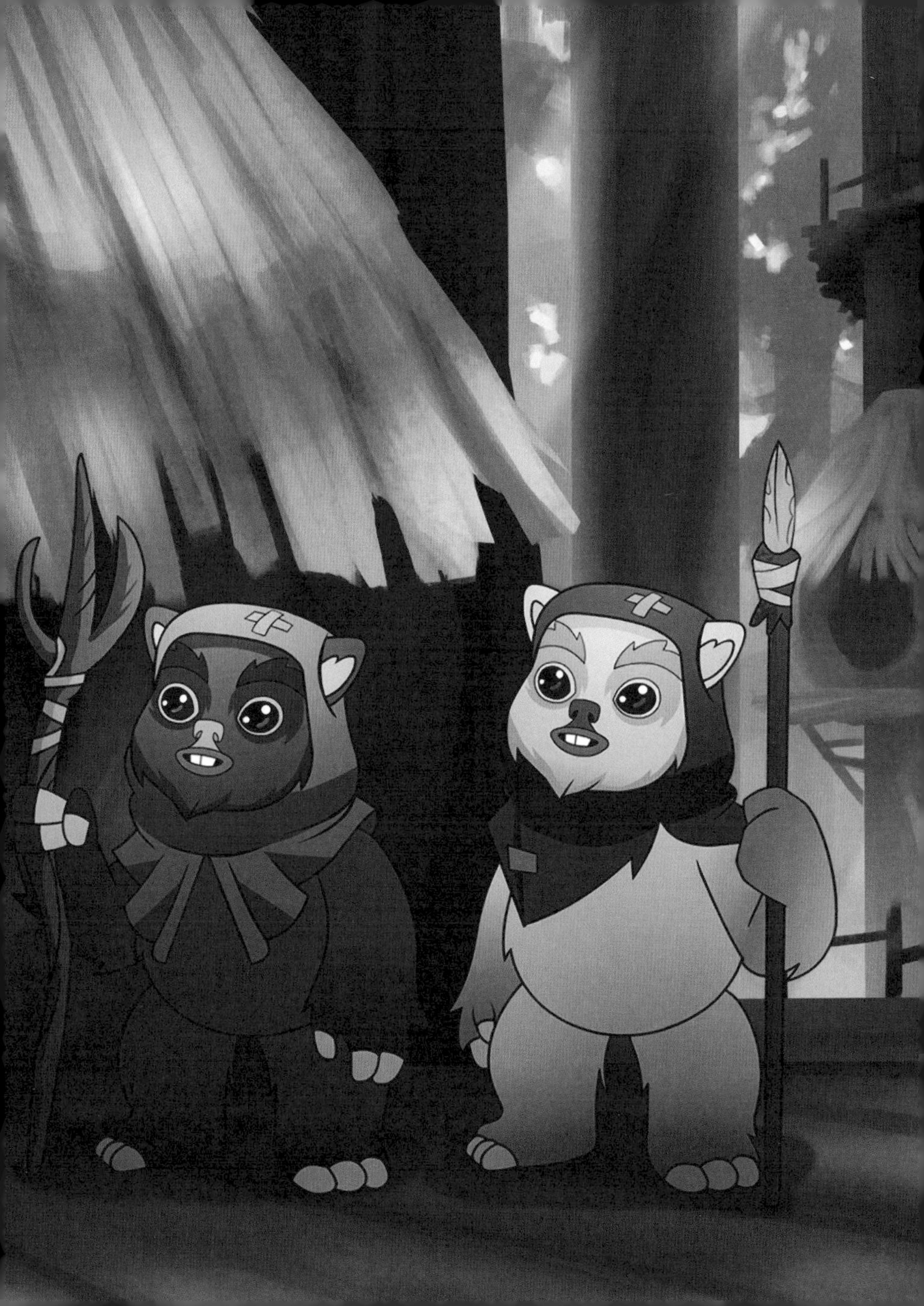

IMPERIAL FEAST

The sounds of the celebration traveled far
through the trees. Fireworks exploded in
the night sky, adding their own colors to the
stardust flung across the heavens, where
X-wings still soared. Leia stood on top of a
boulder and gazed out through the darkening
trees. The Ewoks' celebration fires glowed like

torches in the darkness. Little figures gathered around each one, jumping and dancing, yelling. Their raucous cries matched the feeling in her own heart. The Empire was defeated! She had dreamed of this day—and yet they hadn't gotten where they were with just their dreams. They'd gotten there with wit and cunning and hard fighting.

An Ewok chattered up at her. "Wicket!" She jumped down from the rock and grabbed her friend in a hug, lifting him off his feet and twirling him around. "We've done it!"

Wicket chattered back at her, then embraced her with his stubby arms.

"Your tribe was amazing," Leia said. She knelt and took both of his hands. "Thank you.

We couldn't have done it without you—I mean that."

Wicket nodded seriously, then took her hand, tugging her toward the celebration. Music filled the air as one Ewok beat on three drums strung around his neck. Others blew through horns so big they rested on the ground. At the edges, more Ewoks danced and pounded on big skin drums strung up on low tree branches. Their wild whoops and yells thrilled her and she joined in their dance, holding Wicket's hand and hopping and jumping with them all.

High above them, bonfires roared on the treetop platforms, as if the forest were aflame, and everyone was dancing. Leaving Wicket,

wearing a crown of pine twigs one of the
Ewoks had planted on her head, Leia climbed
one of the rope ladders to the platforms. Han
was up there, and Chewie, and—her heart
leapt—Luke came walking toward her, his face
resigned but triumphant. She grabbed him in a
hug and he squeezed her tight.

Threepio was dancing with Chief Chirpa,
and Chewie and Lando were congratulating
each other. Han was slapping an Ewok on
the back as another one filled his cup from a
skin bag. Leia laughed as a gray Ewok turned
cartwheel after cartwheel. R2-D2 beeped by
her side and she looked down. "My dancing
partner!" she said. "Come here, Artoo." Patting
his dome, she started swaying side to side as

R2-D2 twirled in a circle. Luke laughed and the sound warmed her even further.

Han and Chewie strolled between the fires, Han sipping from a cup of something spicy that one of the Ewoks had pressed on him. It wasn't bad, either. "Well, Chewie, we did it." Han slapped his copilot's hairy shoulder.

Chewie grunted.

"Oh, of course, Chewie—sorry." Han raised his glass in salute. "By the way, stealing that scout walker was a stroke of genius."

Chewie nodded, accepting the thanks. Then

he raised a hand and gestured at a group of stormtroopers, sitting back-to-back with their hands tied behind them. They looked dirty and miserable. Chewie gestured again and growled.

"*What* are the Ewoks doing?" Han looked more closely at the group surrounding the prisoners. They were chanting rhythmically, keeping time with the big drums the shamans were beating, some of them chopping up roots and vegetables on a wide wooden table. As Han watched, three Ewoks drew knives from their belts and began sharpening them on stones while the others looked on approvingly. They kept testing the blades with their fingers, and when they were satisfied, they raised the knives high in the air and shouted something to the others. One Ewok stood right in front of a captive stormtrooper and sliced up an orange vegetable, pelting the trooper with bits of it.

Chewie nudged Han again and grunted.

"Wait . . . wait—the *stormtroopers*?" Han considered. "Well . . . you think we should let them? It's not like the Imperials are our favorite people."

Chewie shrugged.

"Let them what?" Leia asked, coming up behind Han and Chewie.

Han whirled around. "L-Leia! We were just . . ." He looked to Chewie for help.

Leia smiled in a way that said she knew exactly what was going on. "You were just . . . letting the Ewoks cook the enemy?" She shook her head, her smile widening into a grin.

Chewie grunted a defense.

"Don't even try it, Chewie," Leia mock scolded, her hands on her hips.

"We just got here!" Han protested, raising his hands. "How were we to know what they were planning?"

Leia glanced over at the Ewoks happily chopping up vegetables and waving their knives at the stormtroopers. The troopers kept trying to edge away from the Ewoks, sliding centimeter by centimeter across the dirt. "Well, were you going to stop them?"

"Of course!" Han pasted on a look of innocence. Leia narrowed her eyes at him. "Er . . . maybe. Look, who am I to interfere?" He elbowed Chewie, who gave a roar of agreement.

Leia rolled her eyes, but Han could see the

grin she was trying to hide. "I'll take care of this," she said, raising one eyebrow at them.

She turned on her heel and approached the group nearest the stormtroopers. The Ewoks looked up, knives poised. They were almost through the pile of vegetables. The troopers would be next, most likely. She pointed at the prisoners. "Please, let them go." She raised her voice over the music and shouting of the celebration all around them. Overhead, a burst of orange fireworks exploded. "We must treat the enemy fairly." She clasped her hands together pleadingly.

For a long moment, the Ewoks regarded her, knives stilled, and she thought she'd won. One leaned over and jabbered to the others. Leia

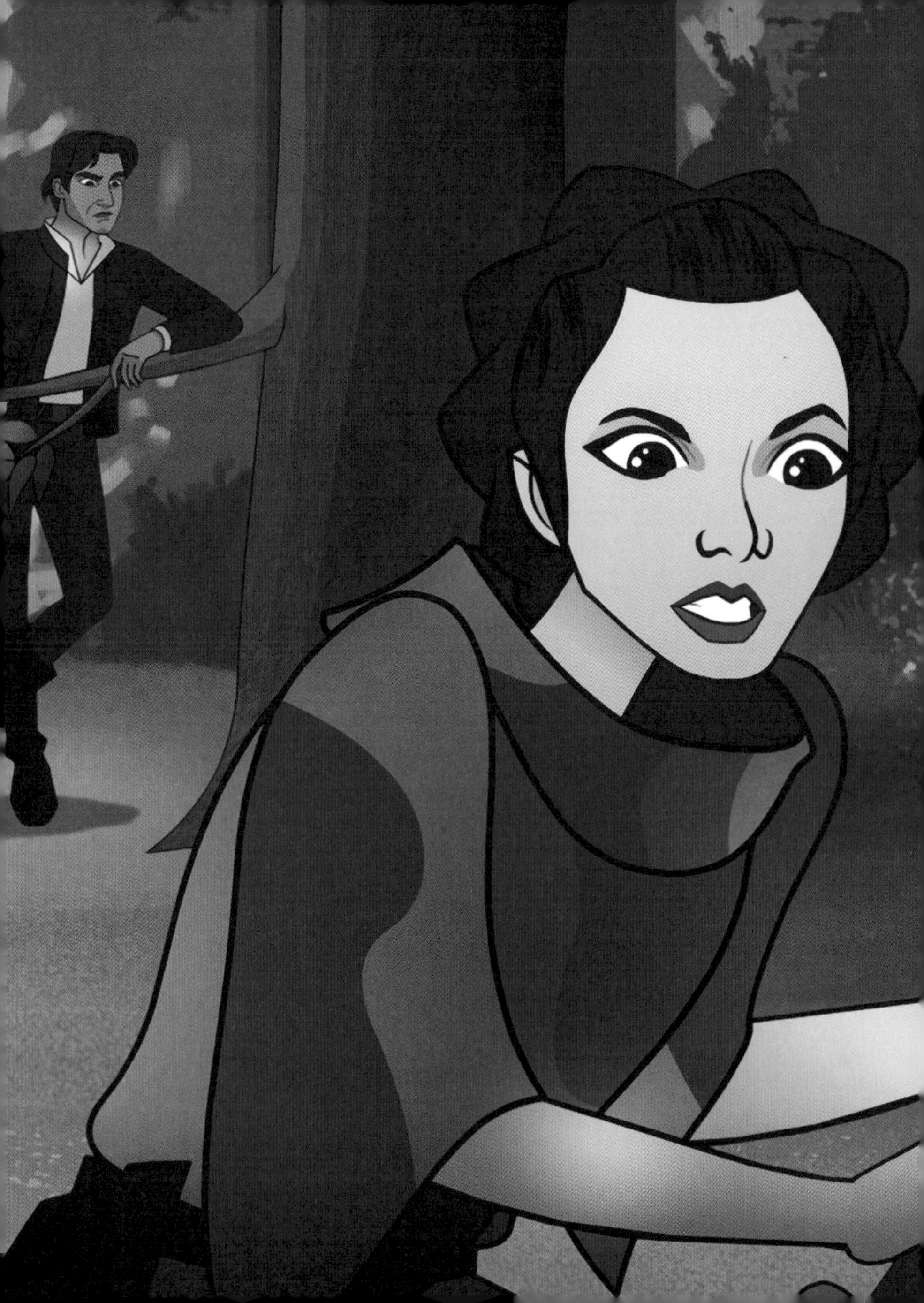

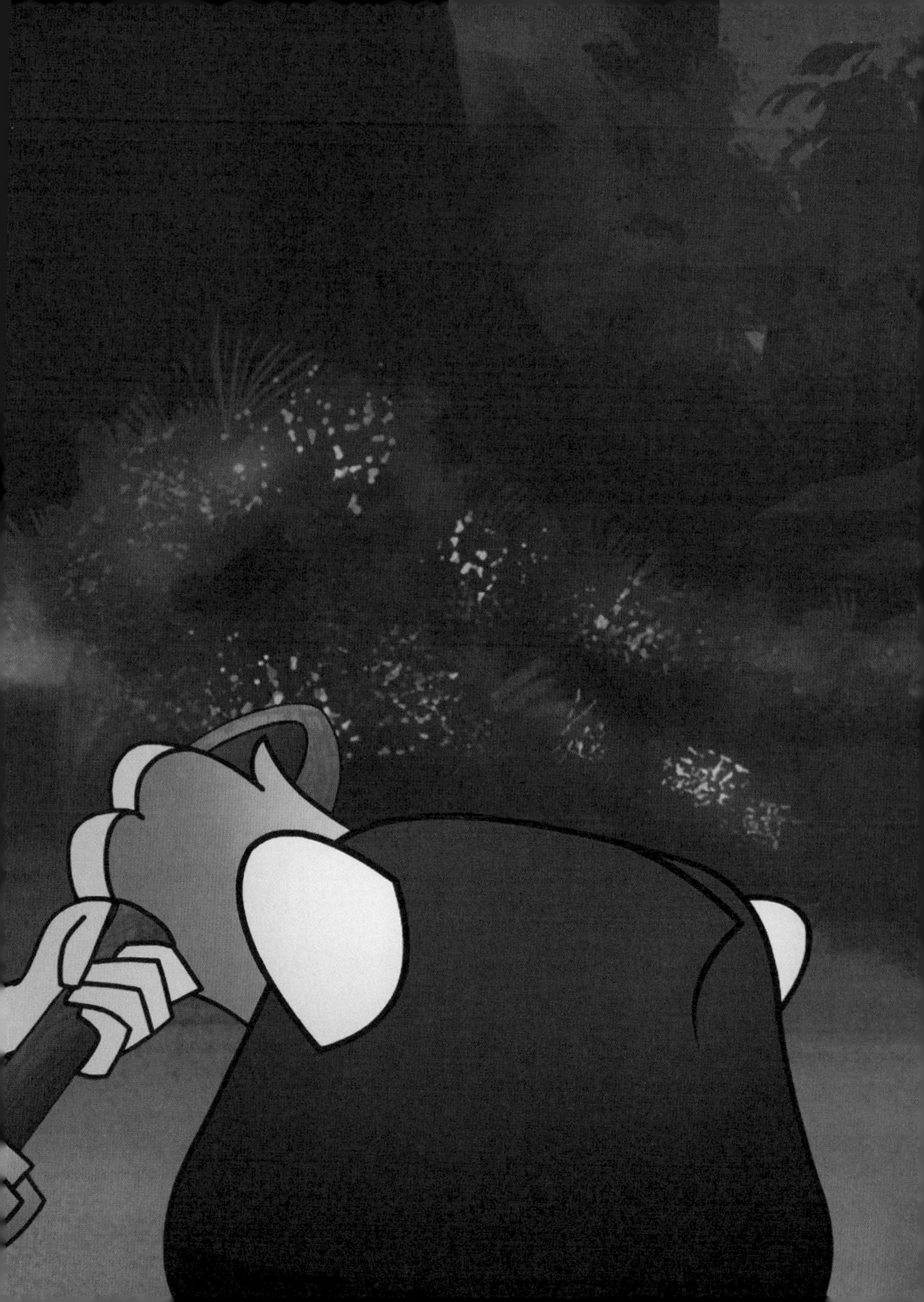

looked around the group. Then they all started chopping again. Leia sighed.

She made her way back over to Han and Chewie. Through the trees she could see Wicket dancing with R2-D2, and C-3PO explaining something to Chief Chirpa with big gestures. "Clearly, the Ewoks are hungry," she said to Han. "Go to General Syndulla's camp and find a crate of ration sticks we can offer them. I'll make sure the stormtroopers stay safe." She gave Han a knowing smile. "Hera will be glad to see you."

"Oh, great. I know what that's gonna cost me," Han muttered. He sighed. "Come on, Chewie. I think I'm going to need some backup here. We better take Artoo, as well."

Chewie grunted.

"Hey, I know, I know. But Leia's right. I guess we have to show the troopers some mercy. Not like they deserve it." He pointed at Leia. "This better be worth it. I'm doing it for you, you know."

Leia rewarded him with a dazzling smile, the kind she knew he couldn't resist. "I know. Thank you."

Hera Syndulla was the captain of the *Ghost*. Han had known her for years; Hera had been with the rebels long before he'd joined. Now she was high up in the Alliance High Command. She was tough, smart, and a talented pilot, he couldn't deny that. The *Ghost* was a modified VCX-100 light freighter, and Corellian like Han's *Millennium Falcon*. Han had seen the *Ghost* in action. The 360-degree dorsal laser cannon turret had taken out plenty of TIE fighters. It was admittedly impressive. But his old ship had done just fine on its most recent mission! Han walked a little faster as he thought of how Lando had flown the *Falcon* into the tunnels leading to the Death Star's reactor core during the battle. The ship had lost its sensor dish, but it still managed to outrun the explosion there at the end. Han could hardly stand that he hadn't been flying it himself, during its greatest moment.

Han strode over to the clearing where the

Ghost and *Falcon* were parked side by side, followed by Chewie and R2-D2. Fires burned there, as well, and joyous shouts echoed among the trees. A knot of rebel soldiers were playing dice in a circle while another group passed a jug from hand to hand, filling and refilling their cups and laughing loudly.

Hera spotted Han immediately. "General Solo!" The green-skinned Twi'lek rose and crossed to Han, standing straight and tall with her shoulders back, as she always did. She put out her hand. "Excellent work today, Solo." The orange-and-white astromech droid Chopper, battered and dirty from the fight, stood next to her, his metal gleaming dully in the firelight.

Han shook her hand. Her grip was firm.

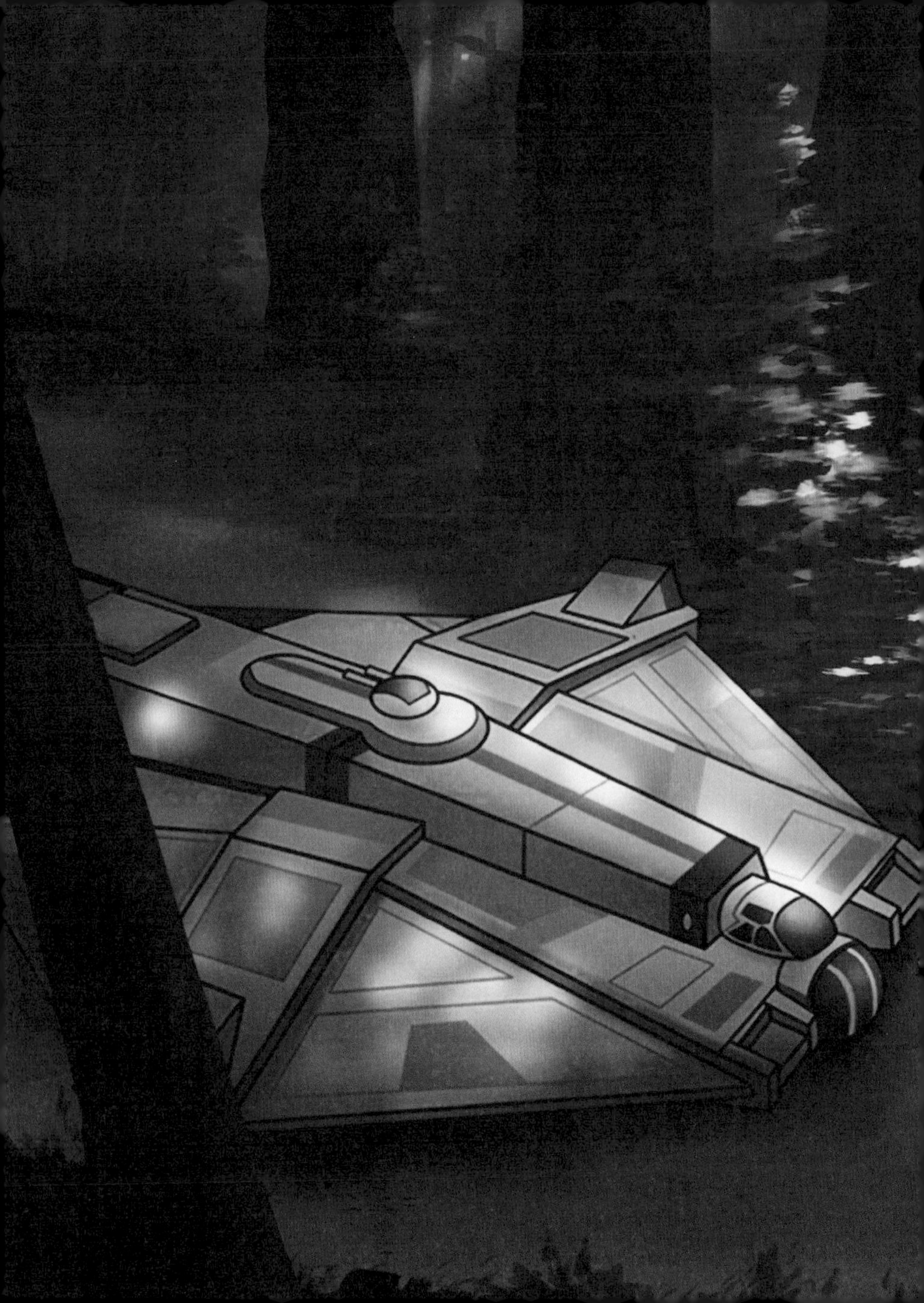

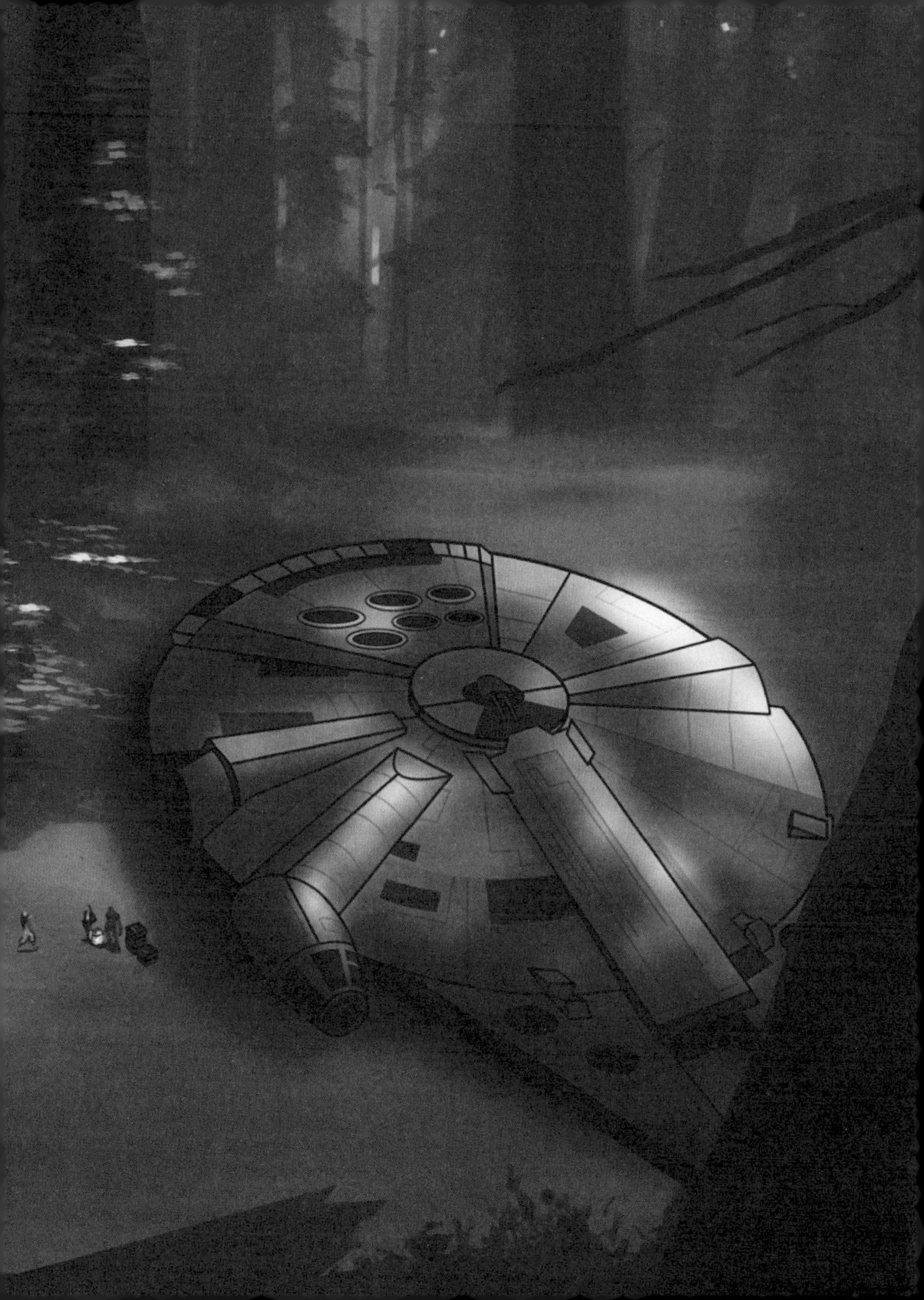

"You weren't bad yourself. I heard the *Ghost* outdid herself up there." He paused and allowed himself a tiny grin. "Still, you just can't beat experience—like the *Falcon.*" Beside him, Chewie barked a laugh.

Hera raised her eyebrows. "Did you want something, Solo, or were you just coming to pay a courtesy call?"

Han wiped off the smile and cleared his throat. "Oh. Yeah. Look, the Ewoks are getting hungry. They're trying to cook up an . . . er . . . *alternative* dinner. And we're hoping to stop them." Hera looked confused. R2-D2 beeped. "Okay, Artoo, I'll get to the point," Han told him. "I know how this sounds, but I need some snacks for the little furballs. They're eyeing the

58

captured stormtroopers, and Leia thinks we should show them some mercy. So we need the ration sticks to trade."

Off to one side, R2-D2 and Chopper were busy with a lively conversation about something, beeping and flashing their lights. A smile spread across Hera's face. She turned

and walked toward a pile of food crates at the edge of the campsite. She turned back toward Han. "I'm glad to give you the ration sticks . . . if you say it."

Han fell back a step. There it was. He knew it! She'd never let it go. He shook his head. All that time—all those years with the Rebellion—all the firefights—and there they were, the Empire defeated and the Rebellion still standing.

Han folded his arms. "I'm not gonna say it."

Hera narrowed her eyes, but the smile was still there, lurking at the corners of her mouth. She shrugged. "Okay, give my regards to General Organa," she said, and started to leave.

Chewie grunted and nudged Han, almost

knocking him off his feet. Han sighed. "All right. Fine!" He raised his voice. "Okay!"

Hera stopped and faced Han. She leveled her gaze at him and put her hands on her hips, tapping her foot. Han cleared his throat. He adjusted his holster belt. He ran his hands through his hair. Then he took a deep breath. "The *Ghost* is superior to the *Falcon*." What were those words that had just come from his mouth? Had he actually said what he'd said?

Hera straightened up. "Well, we finally agree on something." She grinned. "And you can have the rations. Use them in good health."

"Thanks," Han grumbled. Chewie picked up the biggest crate while Hera and Chopper strolled away laughing.

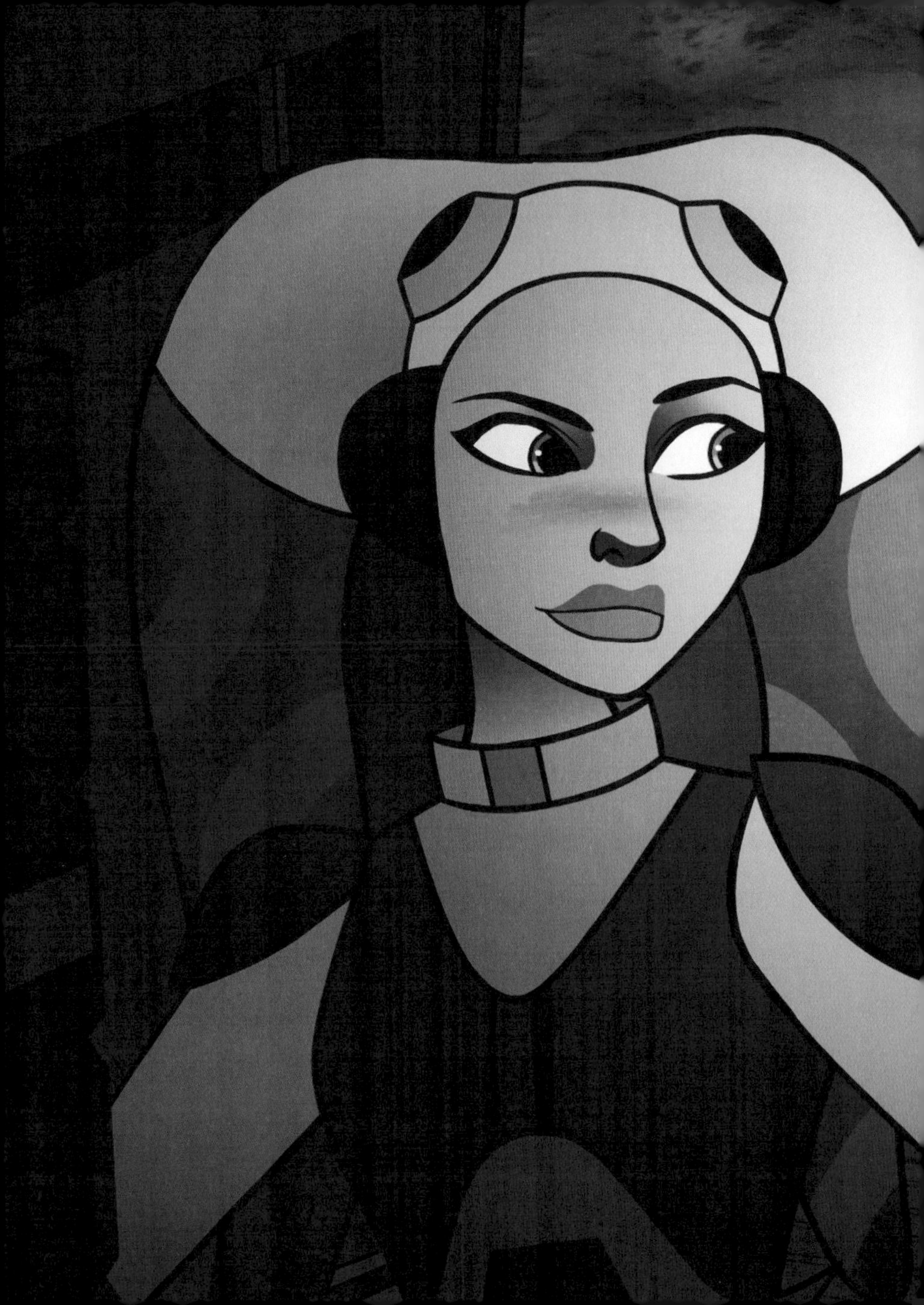

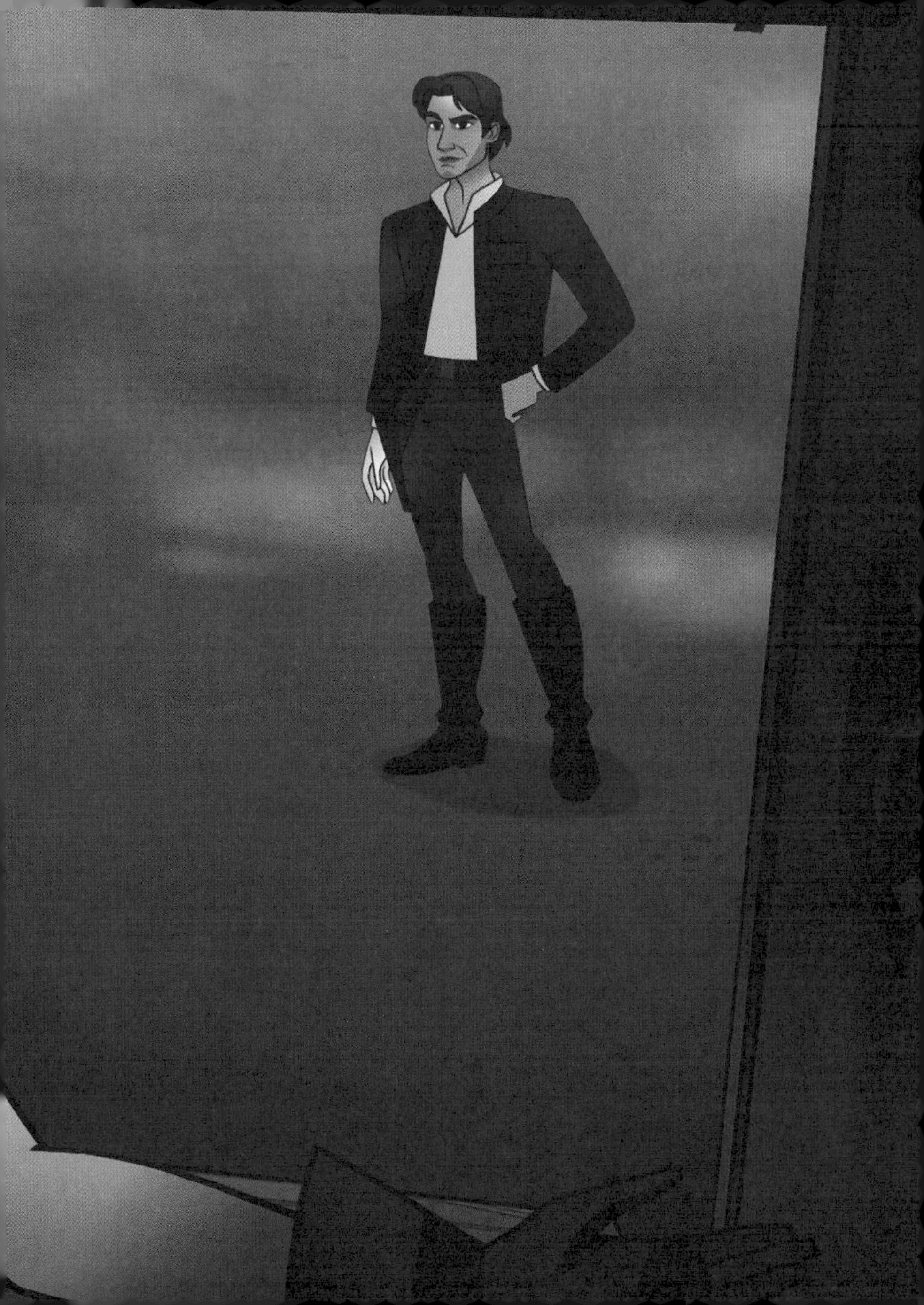

"Please, just wait a little longer," Leia pleaded with the Ewoks surrounding the tied-up group of stormtroopers. The Ewoks chattered and raised their arms. "Food is coming!" Leia told them. "Other food, I mean."

They jabbered at her some more, waving their stone knives. The troopers thrashed in their ropes. "You should be thanking me," Leia said to them over her shoulder. Then Chewie appeared in the light from the fire, and with relief, Leia saw that he and Han were hauling large metal crates. "Finally!" She hurried over to them. "You did it! How was it?"

"Er, okay," Han said. He glanced at Chewie, who growled softly and patted Han on the shoulder.

Leia looked from one to the other. There was something there she wasn't quite getting. But they had the food; that was what mattered. "Everyone! Here!" she called out to the Ewoks, who tottered over. They climbed all over the crates, sniffing them, scrabbling at them, trying to get in. "Hang on, hang on," Leia said soothingly. She pried off one end of a crate, and Chewie picked it up and dumped out the contents. A bunch of ration sticks fell in a pile on the ground.

The Ewoks picked them up, holding them to the light, turning them over in their hands.

Leia knelt in the midst of the Ewoks. She picked up two ration sticks and took a bite of one. "It's food! See, everyone? Food!" She chewed and held out a stick to the nearest Ewok. "Try it." R2-D2 even offered a sniffing Ewok one of the sticks with his metal arm.

Chewie growled as the Ewok regarded the stick in Leia's hand suspiciously. "Oh, she'll convince them," Han replied. "It's hard to resist her. I should know."

The Ewok leaned forward and sniffed the stick. Leia held her breath as he slowly stretched out a hand. He took the stick and carefully bit off the end. No one moved. All eyes were locked on him.

Then he shouted something to the others and, grabbing two handfuls of sticks, thrust his arms in the air. The Ewoks broke into a storm of chattering and swarmed the food pile, shoving the ration sticks into their mouths.

Leia relaxed and heaved a sigh of relief. Han sidled up, looking expectant. Leia patted him on the shoulder. "I'll have to thank Hera for this," Leia said with a grin.

"Hera? What about me?" Han demanded indignantly.

Leia considered him, then smiled. "By the way, nobody believes the *Ghost* is superior to the *Falcon*."

Han exhaled with relief. "Yeah, well, you don't have to tell *me*." He squeezed Leia's shoulder while her laugh echoed through the trees like a bell.

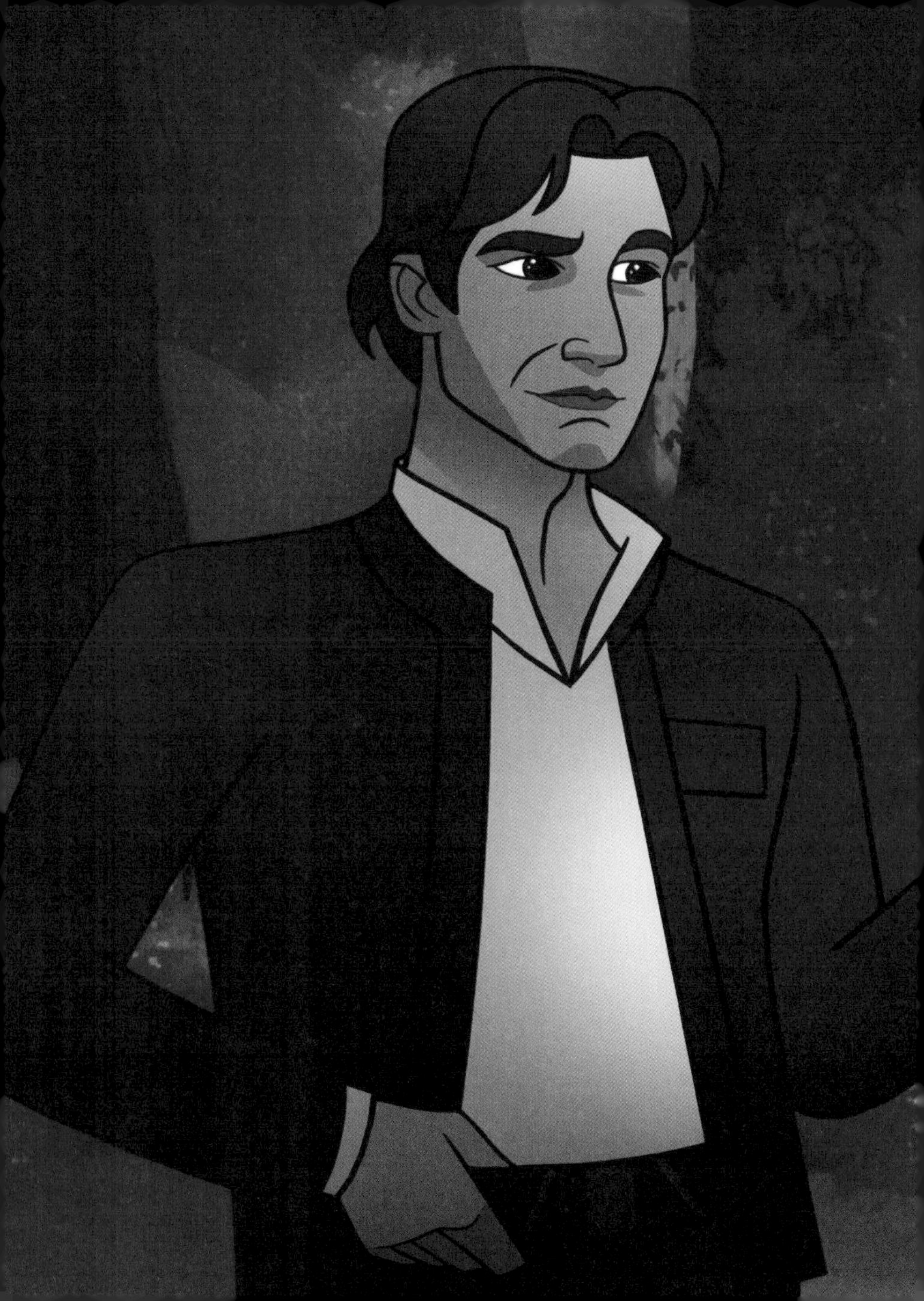

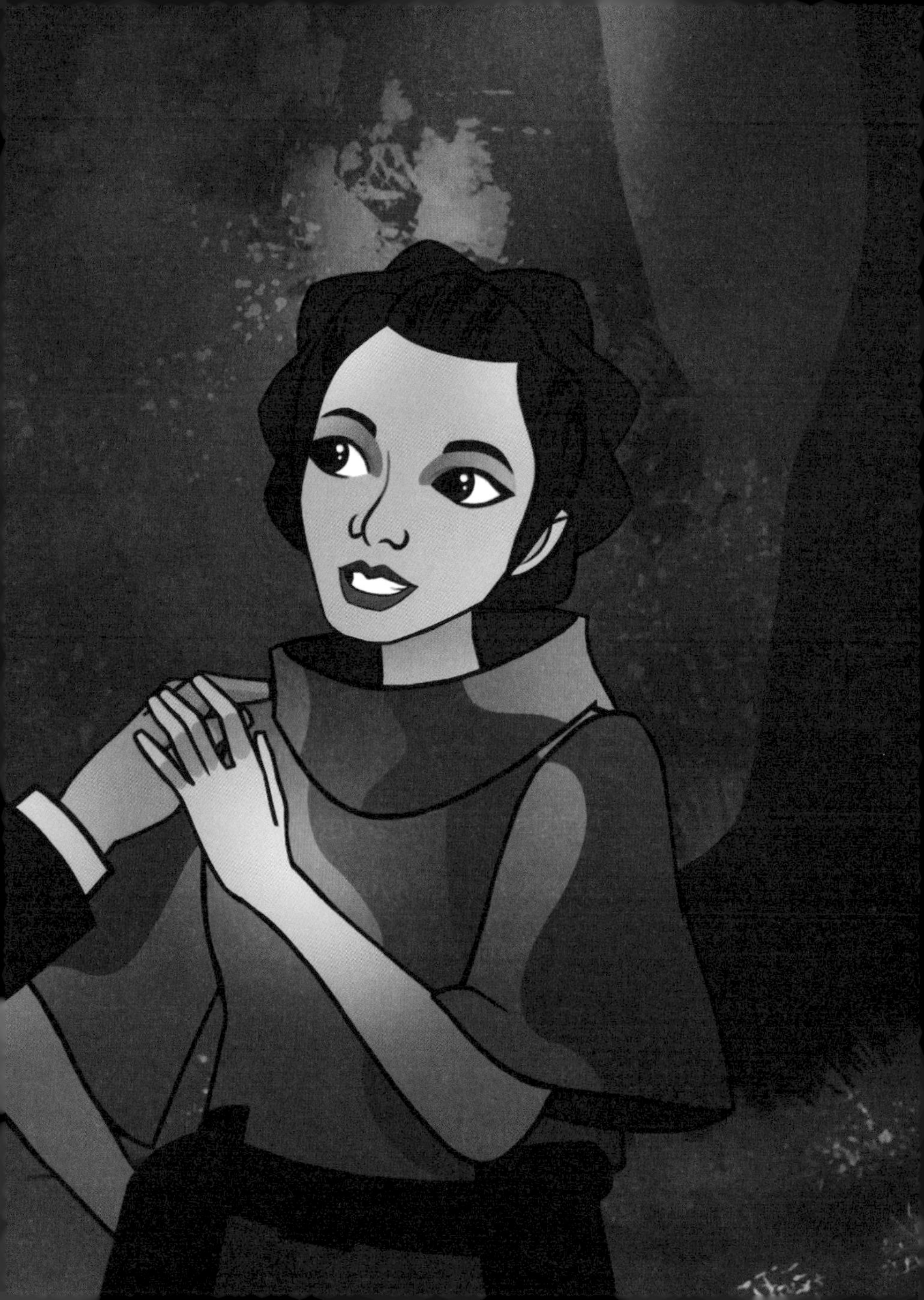

BOUNTY OF TROUBLE

Alone in her quarters on the *Ghost*, Sabine Wren pulled on her jumpsuit and armor. Her stomach felt light and fluttery, the way it always did before a big mission. And that day's mission was big: find Princess Leia Organa in the Garel City spaceport, extract her from her escorts, and obtain the datatape she'd agreed to pass to the Rebellion in her role as a spy.

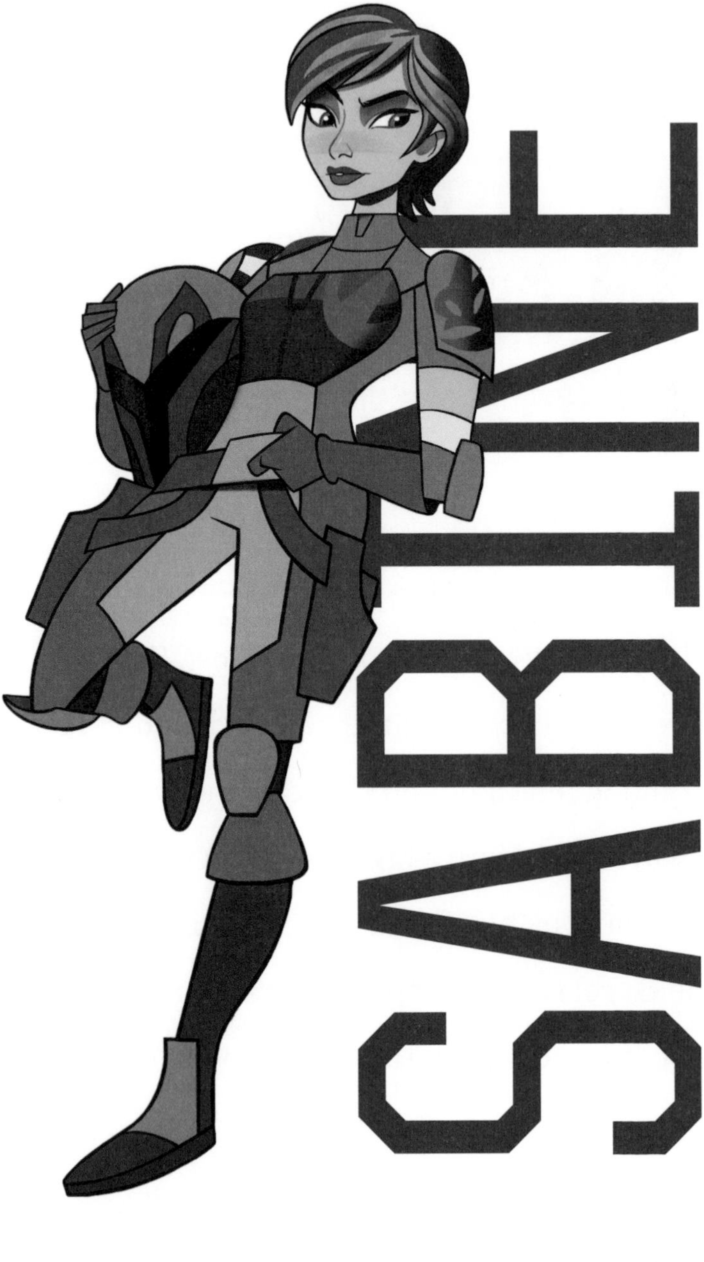
SABINE

Sabine sat at the end of her bunk and pulled on her boots as she considered Leia. Sabine didn't know her very well at all. And she was about to put her life in the princess's hands. If Leia flubbed the mission, if the troopers escorting her got suspicious—well, they'd terminate Sabine faster than she could say "Empire." It was true Leia had basically saved their mission on Lothal with some genuinely quick thinking. It was Leia who'd rallied them when they'd thought extracting their ships from the gravity locks was impossible.

Sabine hung on to that thought as she stood up and took her helmet from the wall. Her hands were sweating. She had to trust Leia. She really had no other choice. The mission timer was ticking, whether she was ready or not.

Princess Leia Organa stared out the window as the Imperial shuttle neared Garel City. The skyscrapers reared their gray heads into the sky. The spaceport was at the center of the city. She drew her hood up around her face and looked carefully at the stormtrooper sitting beside her. Stormtrooper in the front, stormtrooper in the back, two at the controls. They were all supposed to ferry her through the Garel spaceport en route to Coruscant. Except that there would be a little detour along the way, courtesy of Hera Syndulla, Sabine Wren, and Leia. Leia thought of the datatape she'd stashed in the wall terminal in the spaceport. Sabine would intercept their entourage somewhere in the spaceport, and Leia would lead the rebel fighter to the tape. Then Sabine would retreat to the *Ghost* and Leia would continue on to the meeting to discuss the refugee housing situation on Wobani. Leia sighed. Her whole being itched to be out there on the ground, blaster in hand, fighting with the Rebellion. Instead she was skulking around on the inside, pretending to be loyal to the Empire, making nice with the commanders. Still, she *was* working for the Rebellion. She just had to be content working undercover.

The comm crackled to life in the cockpit. "Garel City spaceport approaching, sir."

The pilot commed back, "High-level personage aboard. Secure the area. We will have seven minutes for the mission."

"Sir, will that be enough time?" Leia heard the copilot ask. She could also hear the tension in his voice. They were switching ships to throw off bounty hunters who might have picked up her trail.

The pilot glanced back at her and she met his gaze levelly. He cleared his throat and faced forward again. "The bounty is high on her. We may encounter trouble, so be ready."

The copilot, young and sweaty, nodded. Leia saw his hands white-knuckled on the steering yoke. She smiled to herself. The ship switch was going to give her the perfect opportunity to smuggle the tape to Sabine—bounty hunters or not. Leia looked out the window again. The spaceport was just ahead. She gathered her robes around her. She was ready.

Sabine crept along the wall of the vast Garel City spaceport hangar. Her booted feet slid soundlessly between the crates and boxes that shielded her from the stormtroopers not three meters away. She squinted, blaster cradled in one arm. There she was. Leia wore heavy robes, her face concealed in the hood's deep

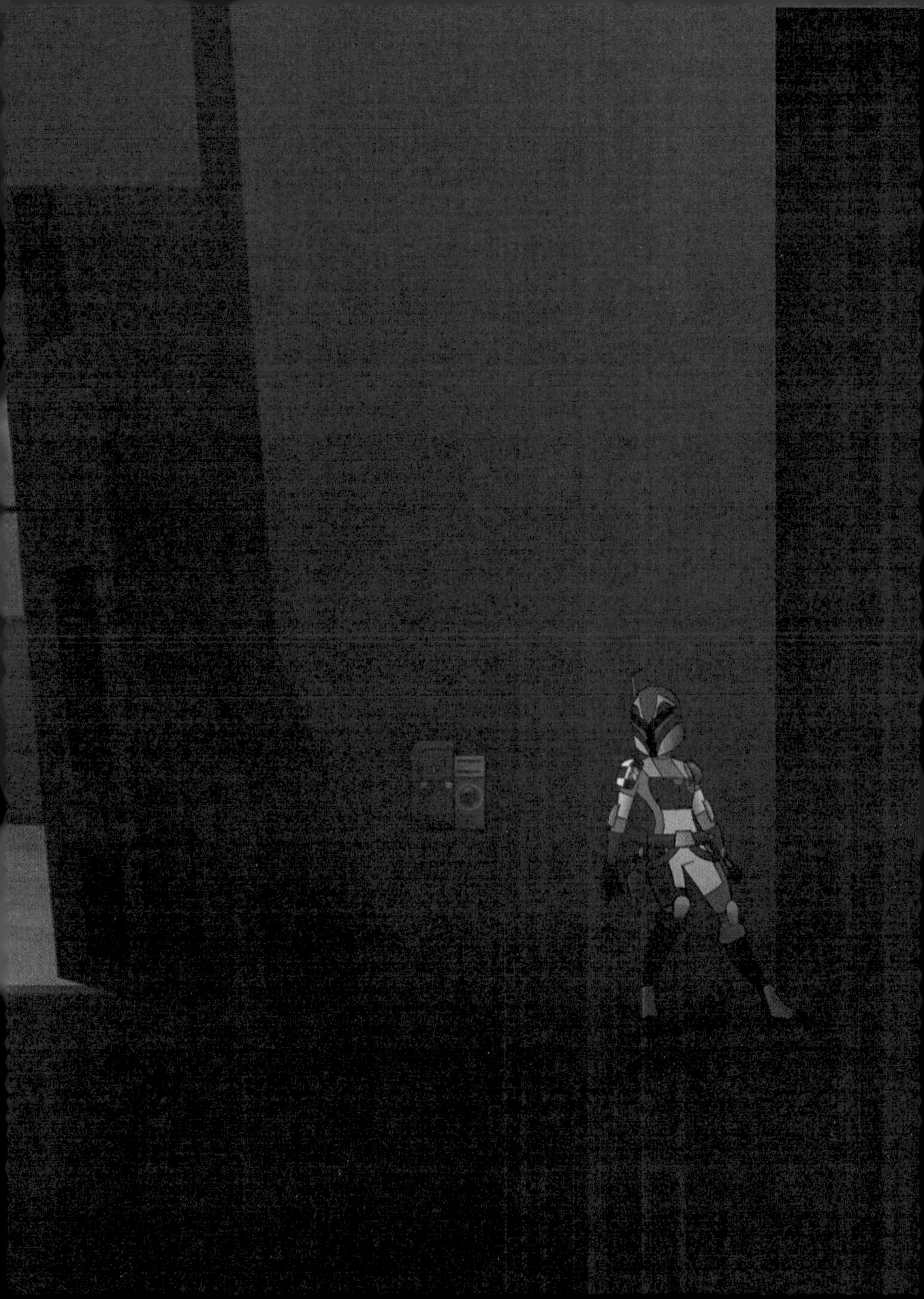

folds. This was going to be a challenge—and Sabine liked a good challenge.

Her comlink crackled on. "Make sure you get the datatape before any real trouble shows up, Spectre-5," Hera said. The *Ghost* was standing ready to extract her as soon as the mission was over.

Sabine thumbed the comlink without taking her eyes off the target. "I'm on it, Spectre-2."

The stormtroopers had reached the access panel at the far end of the hangar. Now was her chance. She had to capture Princess Leia before they took her into the corridor beyond. Running in a practiced crouch, Sabine skirted the walls until she was within bomb range.

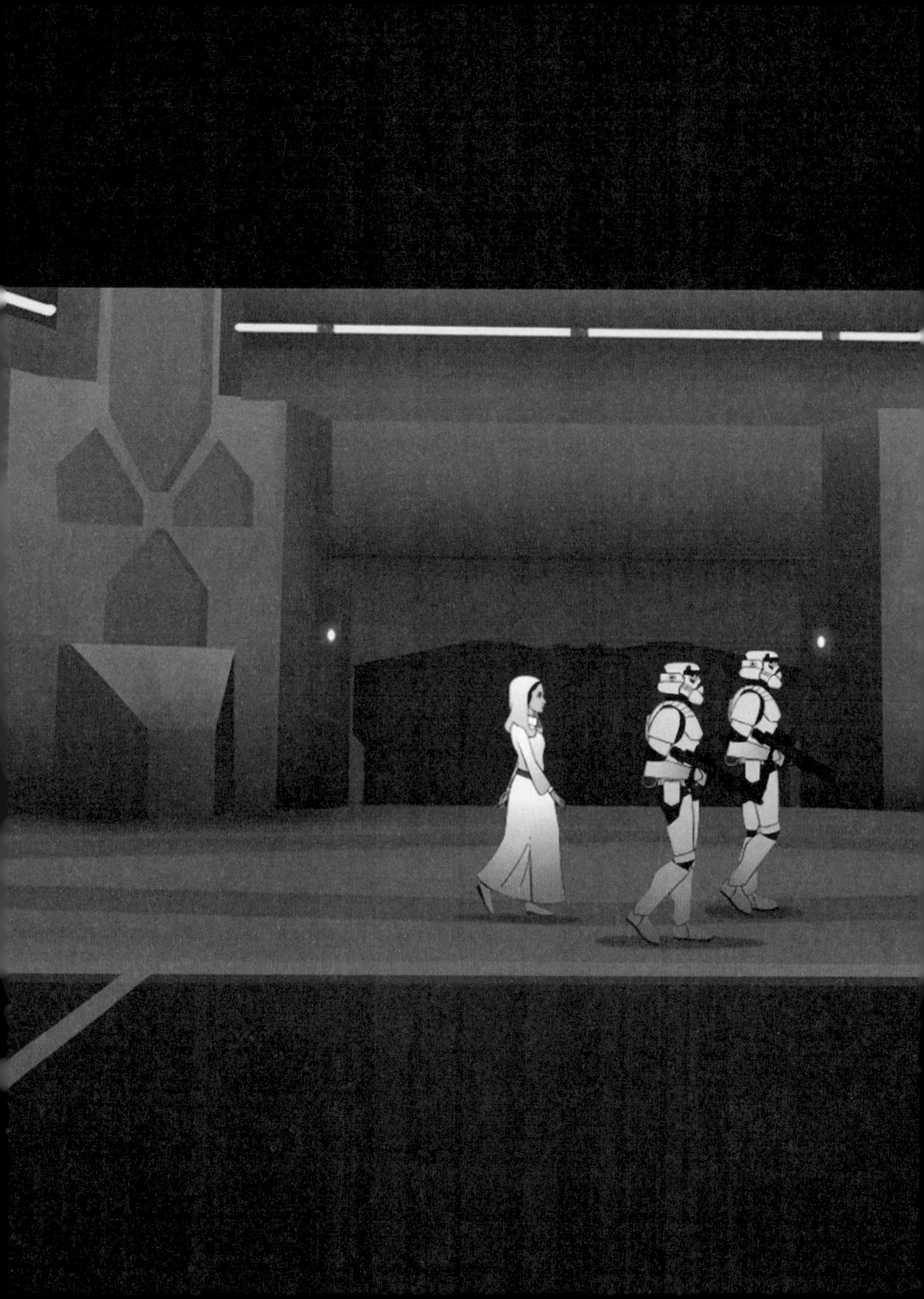

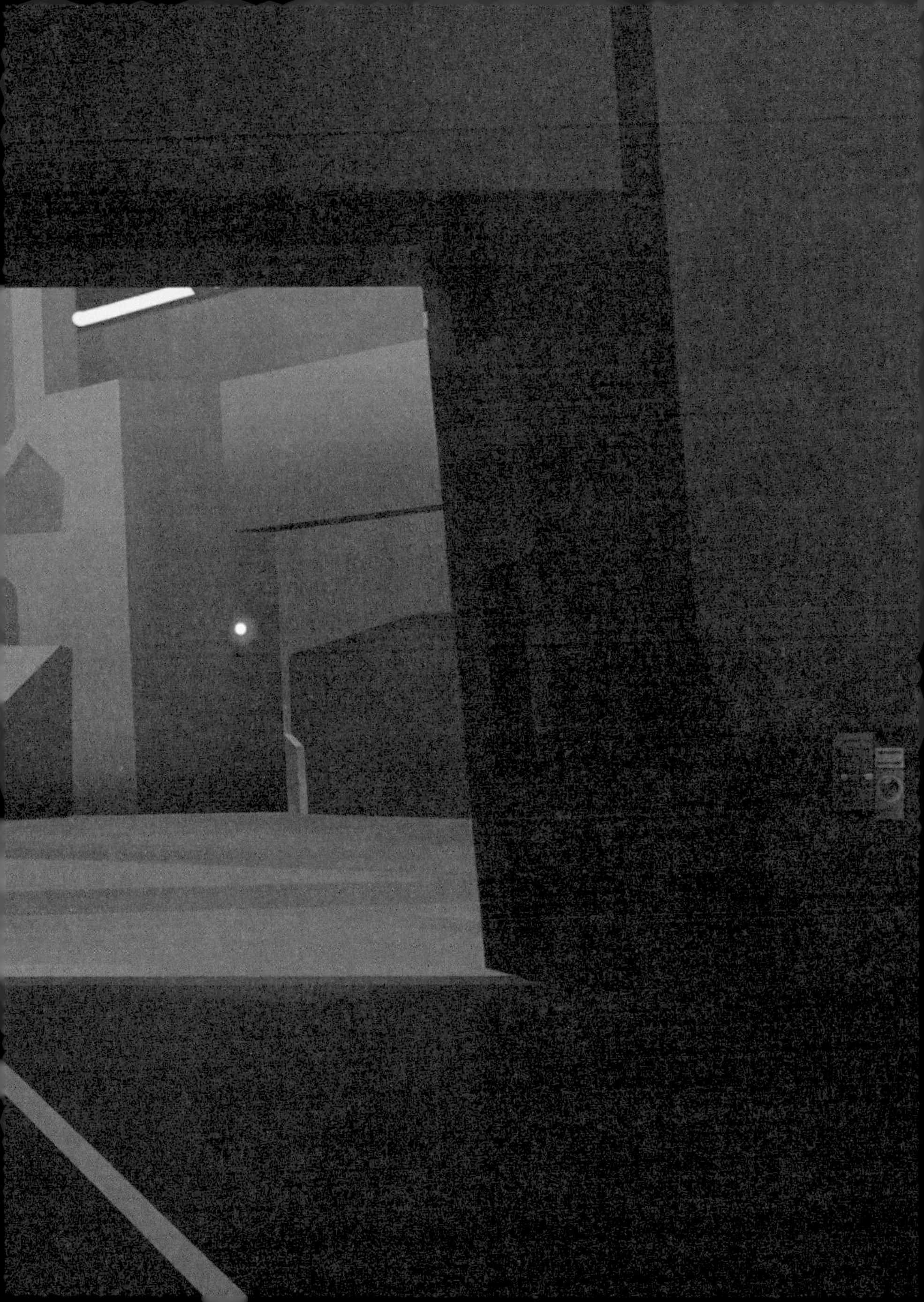

She eyed the troopers, then raised her arm and pitched the bomb into their path.

They grunted and hit the floor, their armor clattering against the metal. "Princess, get back!" one of them shouted, whipping his blaster toward Sabine. Leia spun, her robes swirling around her, and pressed her back against the access panel.

Suddenly, a fibercord shot out. Leia felt it lasso her around the waist, almost knocking her off balance. She was yanked through a doorway. This was it—the figure must be Sabine. She had to make it look real. "Trooper! Help!" Leia yelled, trying to inject fear into her voice.

Before the troopers could react, there was

a massive boom and a dense cloud of yellow paint shot from the bomb on the floor. The troopers yelled as the paint splattered in their faces. Sabine—if that's who it was—dragged Leia backward into a corridor. Sabine blasted the door control panel, and with satisfaction, Leia watched the troopers run toward it as it slid shut in their faces.

"Bounty hunters!" one shouted between coughs. "They've taken the princess!"

The other trooper was looking at his armor. "Is this . . . paint?"

Panting, Leia rested briefly, her back against the cold metal wall. The rebel took off her helmet. Blue hair, sharp eyes. It was Sabine, all right. She stuck out her hand. "Hi!

I'm Sabine Wren. I was sent here to capture you. Do you have the datatape?"

"Yes," Leia said. "I had to hide it though, so the Imperials don't know I'm working for the Rebellion."

A crash came from the other side of the door and the control panel flickered. The troopers were trying to break through.

Sabine replaced her helmet and ran Leia down the corridor and into another one, lined with pieces of machinery.

"This way!" Leia called to Sabine. "I hid it in this panel." She pulled the cover off and removed the tape. "Here. The datatape of the Imperial base locations. Use it well." She held Sabine's gaze.

But before she could hand off the tape, a humanoid figure loomed at the end of the corridor. Metal creaking and lights blinking, it stomped toward them.

Leia's eyes widened. "What is *that*?"

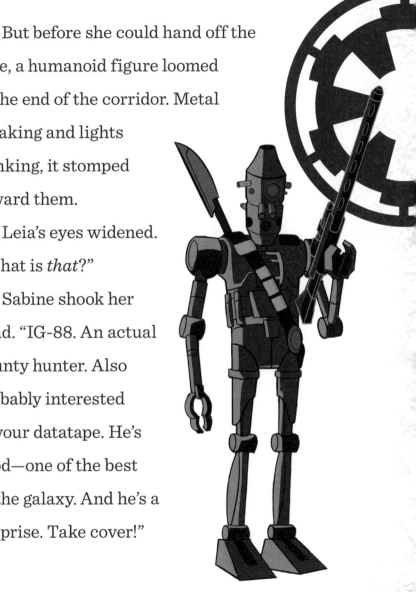

Sabine shook her head. "IG-88. An actual bounty hunter. Also probably interested in your datatape. He's good—one of the best in the galaxy. And he's a surprise. Take cover!"

They both dove for a doorway as the droid opened fire. "What's the plan?" Leia panted, pressing herself against the shallow opening. "You strike me as the type of woman who usually has a plan."

"No fear. I do have a plan." Sabine pulled a paint bomb from her belt. She only had one left though. And if it didn't work—well, she was good with a blaster. But IG-88 was good, as well. "Hang on." She slammed the bomb against the metal wall, where it stuck and started ticking. The droid walked toward them, its metallic footsteps magnified in the tubelike metal corridor. Red blaster fire zinged around them. Closer. Just a little closer and the droid would pass the bomb.

Boom! The bomb exploded, showering the droid in purple paint.

"Go, go!" Sabine shouted.

They skidded to a halt in front of the jammed door. Screeching metal signaled that the troopers were almost through. "Hide!" Leia hissed.

Sabine darted behind a pile of boxes. The screeching noise grew louder and a section of the metal door thunked to the floor as the troopers cut their way through. "There she is!" one of them shouted. "Senator! Are you unharmed?"

Just then, IG-88 clumped into the corridor, straight toward Leia—and the doorway blocked by troopers. Leia looked from the droid to

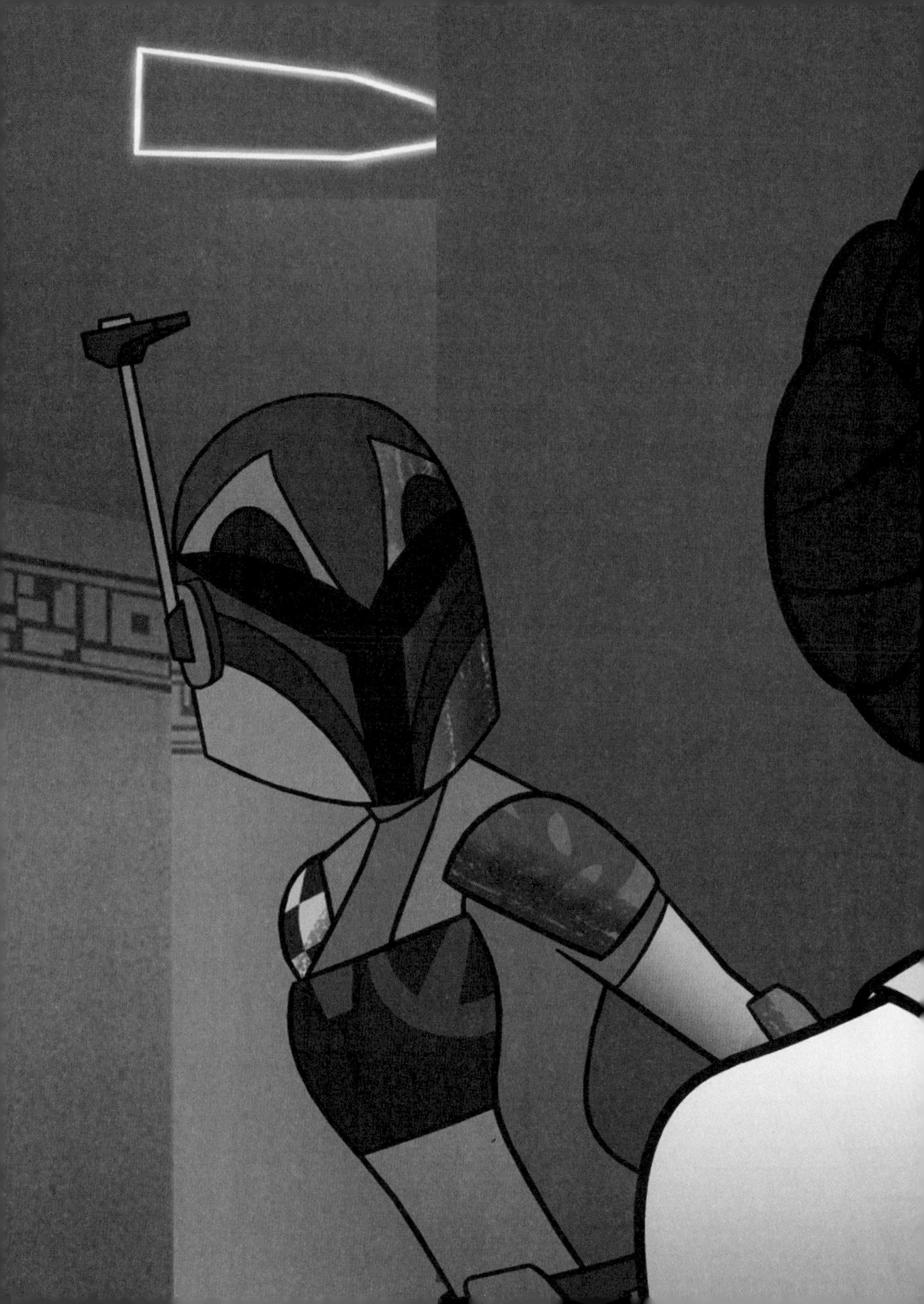

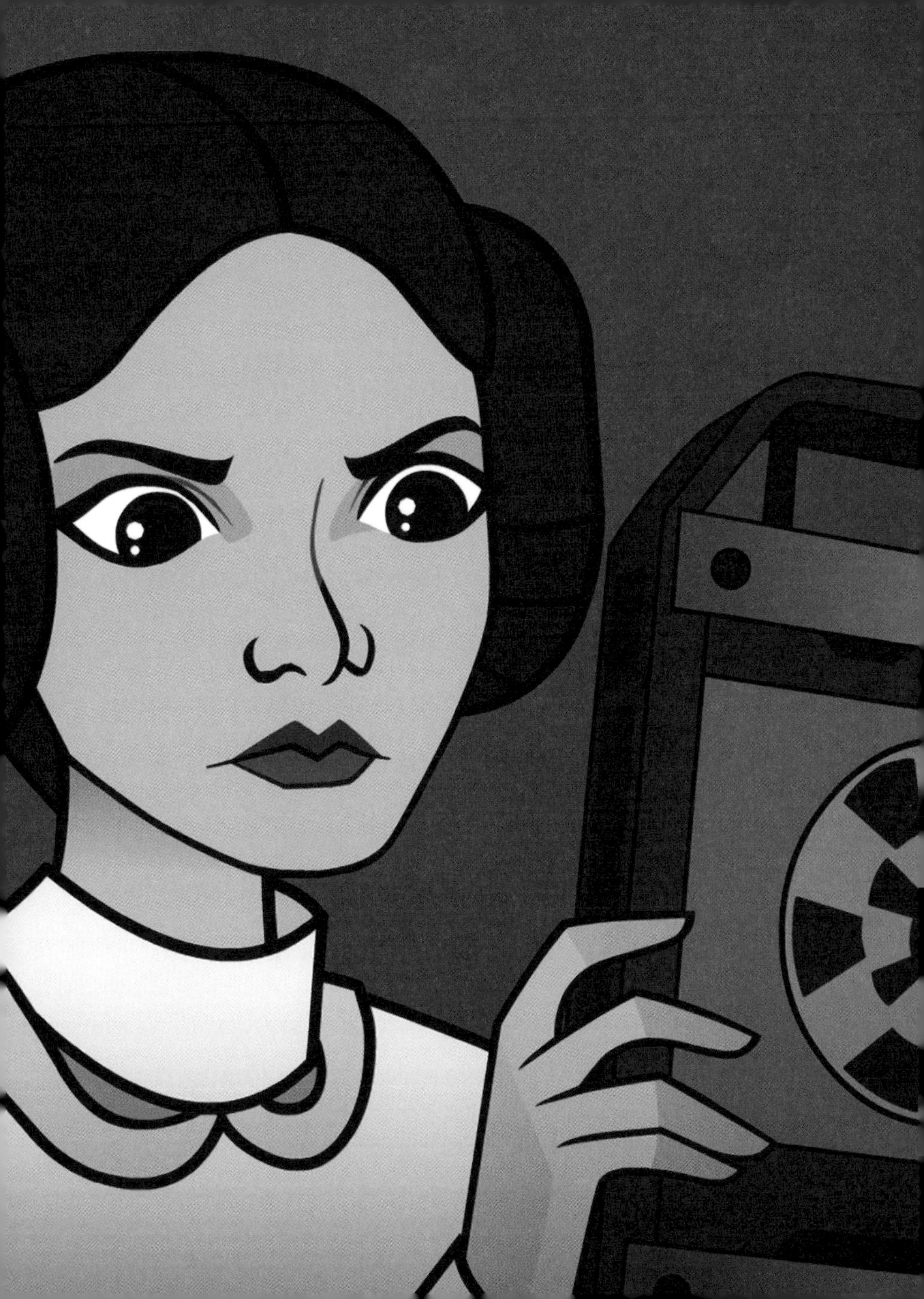

the troopers and her eyes narrowed. Sabine suddenly saw Leia's plan as clearly as if she'd drawn it out.

"It's about time! Blast that bounty hunter!" Leia shouted, pointing at IG-88. The troopers immediately fired, their blaster bolts ricocheting off the droid's armor. The droid stomped forward inexorably, blasting the troopers in return. One of them hit the floor, groaning. The other flew back over some crates, thrown by the force of IG-88's blasts.

"Come on!" Leia said to Sabine. Under cover of the chaos, Sabine slid from behind the crates and ran after Leia down a corridor to the right.

Halfway down, Leia stopped and caught her breath. She pushed her hood back and wiped her forehead. "I have to go back before they realize I'm missing again." She handed the tape to Sabine, holding her gaze.

Sabine nodded. "This means a lot to the Rebellion. Thank you, Senator Organa." She paused. "I mean, Princess—no, I mean—"

Leia placed her hand on top of Sabine's. "*Leia.*"

"Leia," Sabine repeated.

Leia glanced back down the corridor. The shouts of the fighting echoed through the doorway. "I better go back now." She turned away.

Sabine watched her run lightly down the hall, robes billowing behind her. "Leia!" she called suddenly.

The princess turned back.

"You keep fighting on the inside, I'll keep fighting on the outside."

Leia smiled. Her eyes met Sabine's again—fighter to fighter. "I hope one day we can fight together." She raised her hand and tipped Sabine a salute. Then she disappeared through the opening.

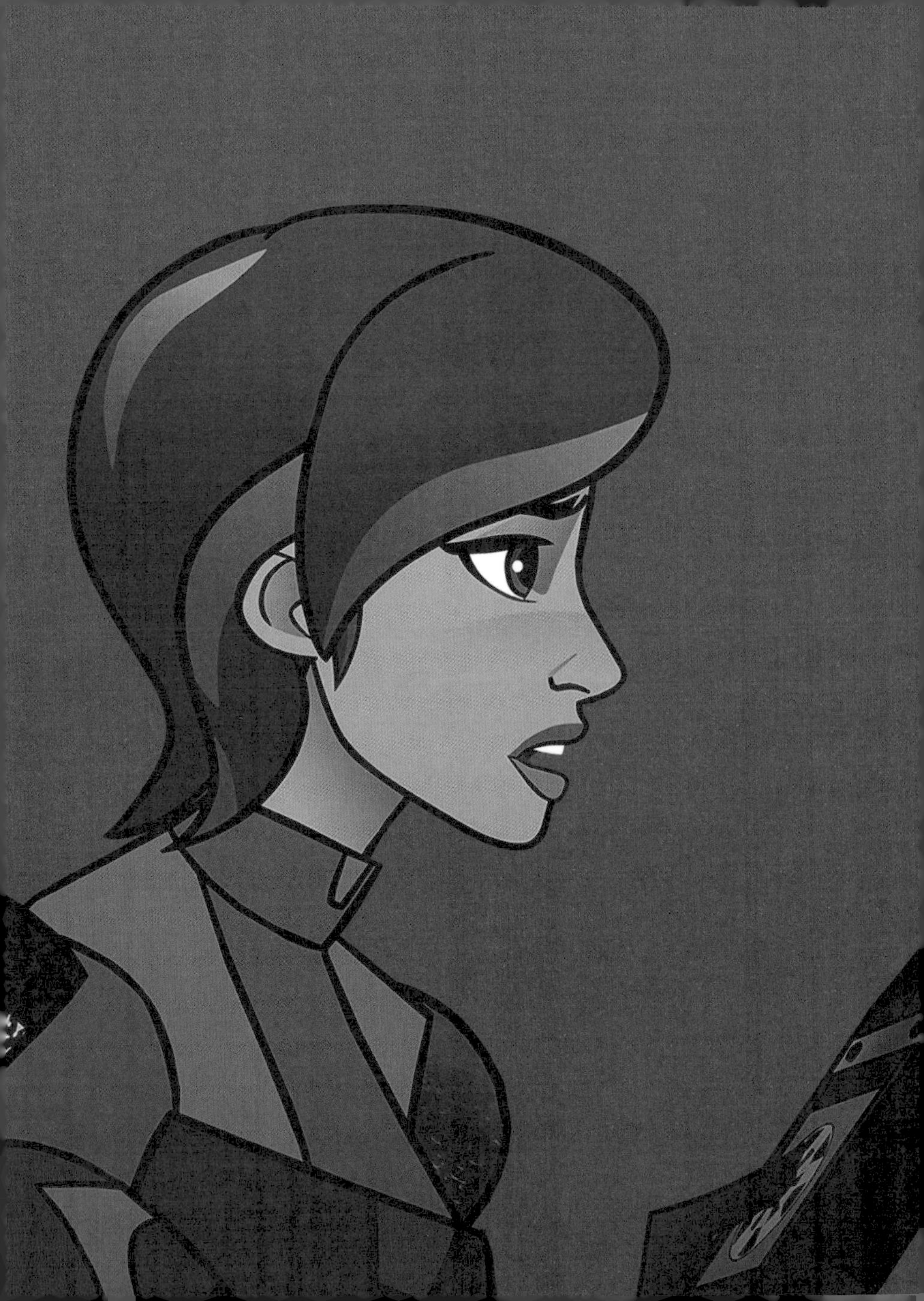

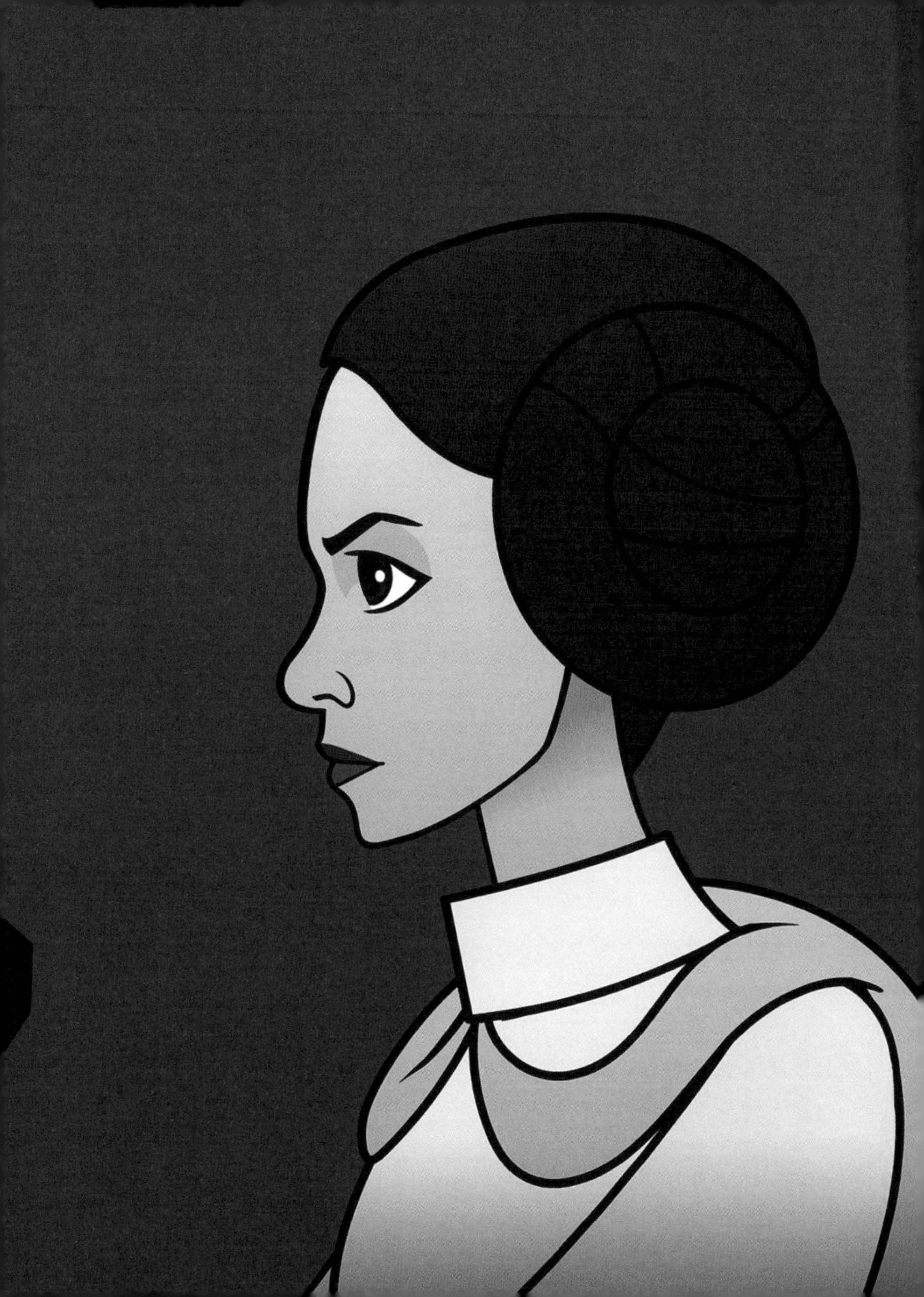

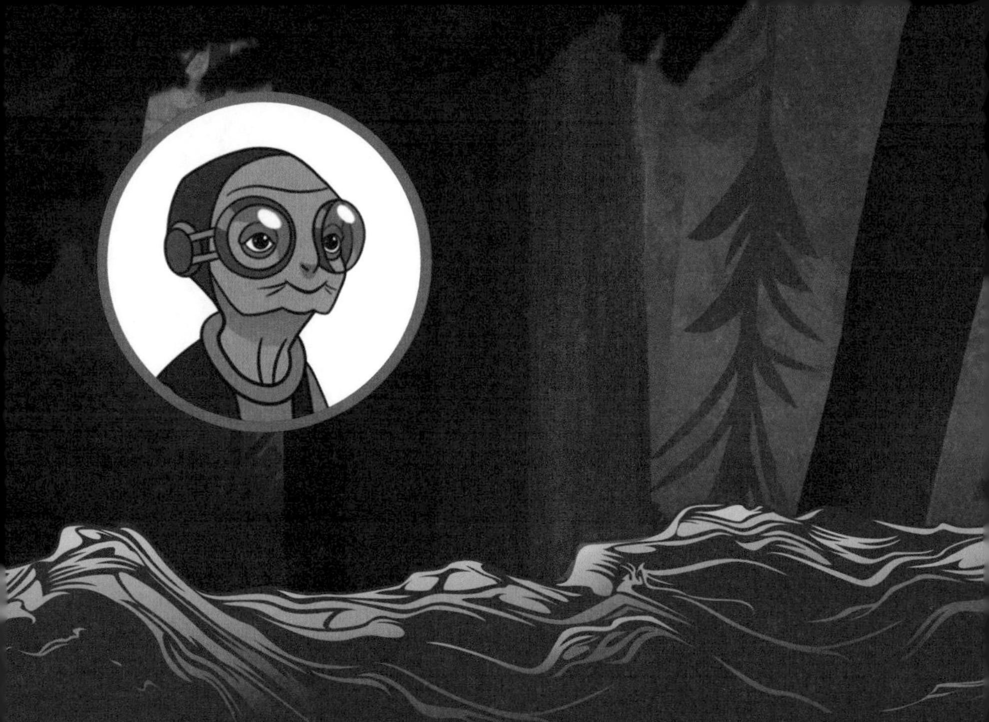

A Message from Maz

Do you feel the spray of the water? Can you see how it crashes over the rocks in the light of the torch? I am glad you are sitting with me, here on this damp grass. You trusted me—and now we are friends, aren't we? That is good. Friends carry me through my days. They have

carried me through my life. You have found that, too, haven't you? Friends fight *for* us and they fight *with* us. We want to be heroes—and with friends, we always are. Friends are heroes to each other. And we see that as strong as we thought we were alone, we are stronger with our friends. And sometimes we need to humble ourselves before our friends, too. Friends bring out these good qualities in us—these qualities that make a hero, you might say. You know that

now. By letting go, we will be more like the river: flexible, everlasting, and always flowing ahead. Gentle sometimes, powerfully angry other times. Hold the torch up. See how the light glows on the water. I am glad you have come to talk with me. I see that you must go. I understand. But remember—find friends wherever you go. They will bring out the hero in you. And safe journey.

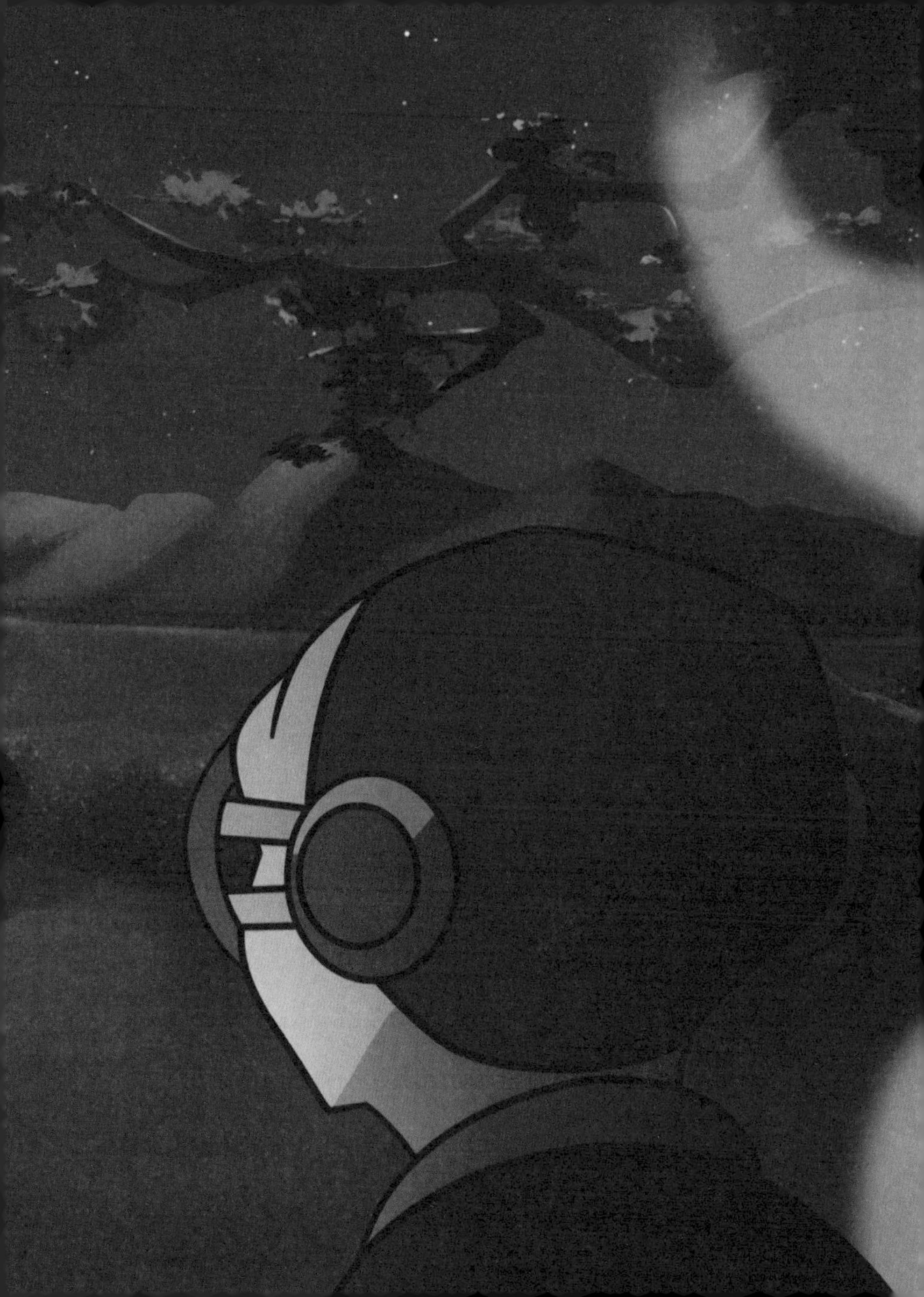

ABOUT THE AUTHOR

EMMA CARLSON BERNE has written many books for children and young adults, including historical fiction, sports fiction, romances, and mysteries. She writes and runs after her three little boys in Cincinnati, Ohio.

STAR WARS
FORCES OF DESTINY™

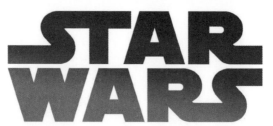

COLLECT THEM ALL!

Set of 4 Hardcover Books ISBN:
978-1-5321-4324-3

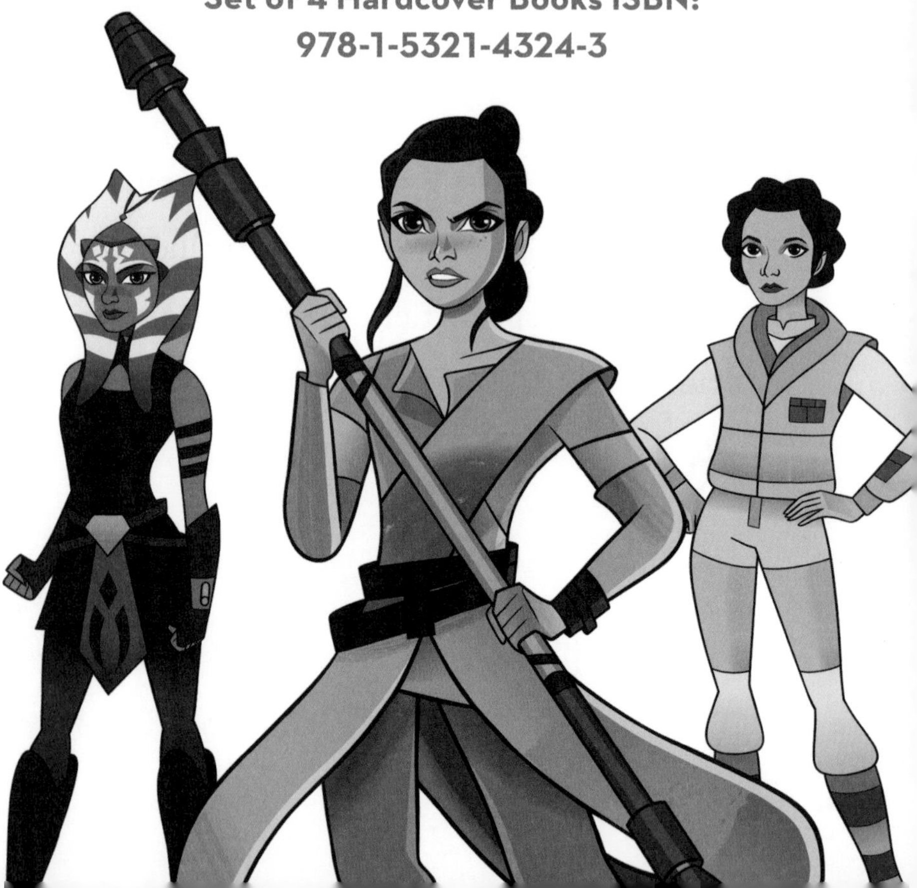

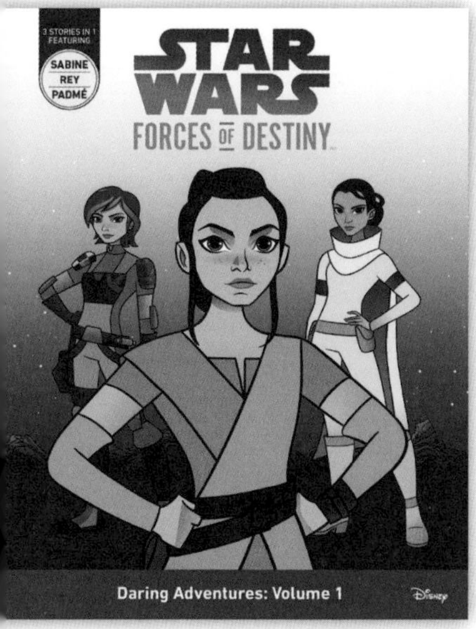
3 STORIES IN 1 FEATURING
SABINE
REY
PADMÉ
STAR WARS
FORCES OF DESTINY
Daring Adventures: Volume 1
Disney

Hardcover Book ISBN
978-1-5321-4325-0

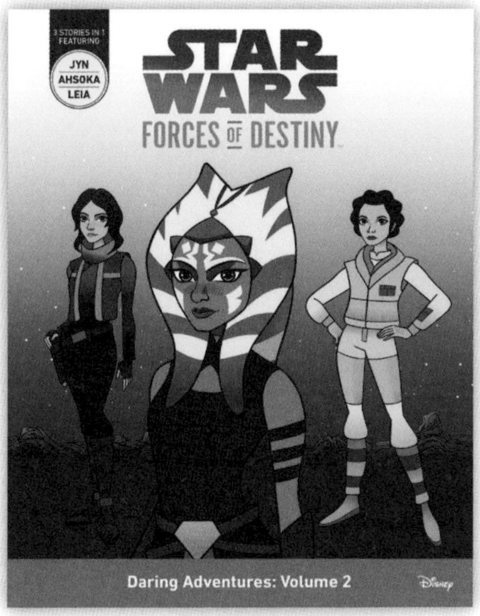
3 STORIES IN 1 FEATURING
JYN
AHSOKA
LEIA
STAR WARS
FORCES OF DESTINY
Daring Adventures: Volume 2
Disney

Hardcover Book ISBN
978-1-5321-4326-7

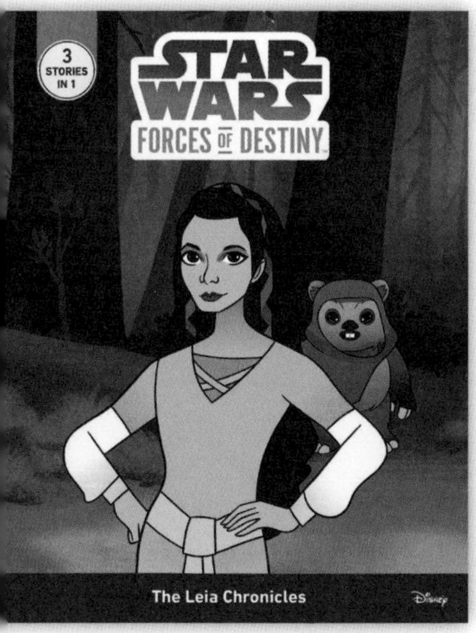
3 STORIES IN 1
STAR WARS
FORCES OF DESTINY
The Leia Chronicles
Disney

Hardcover Book ISBN
978-1-5321-4327-4

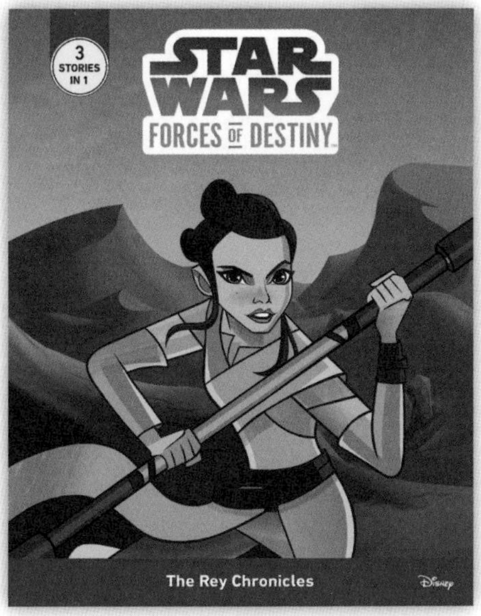
3 STORIES IN 1
STAR WARS
FORCES OF DESTINY
The Rey Chronicles
Disney

Hardcover Book ISBN
978-1-5321-4328-1